NØKKEN

UNDRALAND
BOOK TWO

MARY E. TWOMEY

MARY E. TWOMEY, LLC

Nøkken
Book Two in the
Undraland Series

By

Mary E. Twomey

COPYRIGHT

Copyright © 2015 Mary E. Twomey
Cover Art by Crowe Covers
Author Photo by Lisabeth Photography

All rights reserved.
First Edition: May 2015

This is a work of fiction. Any resemblance of characters to actual persons, living or dead, is purely coincidental. The author holds exclusive rights to this work. Unauthorized duplication is prohibited.

This book is licensed for your personal enjoyment only. If you would like to share this book with another person, please purchase an additional copy for each reader. Thank you for respecting the hard work of this author.

For information:
http://www.maryetwomey.com

DEDICATION

For Sunday

*Carve your own path that leads you
to be a leader, a blessing, and a compassionate caregiver
to those less fortunate than you.*

HAZE, HALFY AND HIM

Tor's booming voice infiltrated my delirium. "I know, but we have ta get moving. They'll wise up and search the mountains fer us soon. How well do ya think they'll fare then?" I could picture his red face and ratty dreadlocks as he spoke. We were on the mountain, still tucked in the cave after Jamie and I had killed a Werebear together. We were sick with some awful virus that I prayed would pass before I ralphed again. I had nothing left in my stomach, but the green around the gills feeling was still lending its oppressive vibe.

Jens argued, "But their fever's not even broken yet! Moving them now? I don't like it."

"It don't matter whatcha like. Lucy and Jamie'll be easy targets when scavengers come fer this dead Werebear."

Foss chimed in, "Which could be any moment, mind you. Take the prince, leave the rat. I'll buy you a new one."

"But what happened?" Britta demanded an answer. "She's got a couple bruises, but that's it."

Charles sounded grim. His words delivered a weighty blow I was too much a foreigner to properly understand. "There's no way she and Jamie could be exactly this sick out of nowhere at the same time."

"If you want me to say it, I won't. It's impossible," Jens ruled.

"There's a dead Were right in front of your face, Jens." Mace lowered his voice. "You know what this is. You just won't admit it."

"There's nothing to admit! She's a pacifist. There's no way she could have killed that Were with Jamie. You don't know her like I do."

"Maybe *you* don't know her as well as you think you do," Mace countered, playing the antagonist. "It's obvious to everyone but you that she laplanded with Jamie."

Jens lashed out at Mace. "Hey, newbie. Why don't you shut your trap and make yourself useful helping Britt and Alrik with the stretcher?"

I wanted to get up and join them to see what I'd missed, to tell Jens and Mace to stop fighting, but my body was uncooperative. I could crack one eye open, but that was all. The rest of me was totally useless.

I'm sure there was more talk happening, but I couldn't understand a lick of it as my brain floated in and out of consciousness. The next thing I registered was being picked up and laid somewhere cold and sweaty and hairy -

Jamie. There was a faint notion that I was somehow floating with him on a stretcher of some sort, but I was too out of my body to investigate further.

After that, I have no idea how much time passed or what happened. All I could hope was that Jens was nearby to keep my useless body from further harm.

DAYLIGHT FELT WARM ON MY SKIN AFTER THE... NIGHT? Week? Month? I'd been cold. I turned over on my side and snuggled into the growing warmth next to me, wrapping my arms and legs through it contentedly.

I inhaled the scent of oatmeal cookies.

Ah, Jens. My guardian garden gnome I hadn't actually known all that long. Now, despite the arguing, I was growing attached to him in a way I was not quite ready to examine. I missed sleeping next to him, even though we'd only done that once.

I nuzzled his neck with my nose and planted a kiss on a sensitive spot I knew would make him tingle. Before we could get into another fight, I wanted to enjoy the peace of his protection.

"Uh, Lucy? What are you doing?"

"I missed you, Jens." I murmured sleepily.

"Did you, now?"

His teasing voice was a sweet sound to the nothing I'd been processing for this elongated period of time. It sounded far away, but still somehow near, like I was hearing him through water. As my senses began coming back to me, I realized that his voice was coming from somewhere behind me.

My eyes flew open, and I found that the warmth I was kissing was not Jens, but Jamie.

I should've known. Jens smelled like a warm sugar cookie, not an oatmeal raisin.

I fumbled backwards on the bed in confusion. I tried to jerk myself up, but my muscles were out of practice. I groaned when my neck cracked without my permission. "What the... Where am I?" Before I could get an answer, I started coughing. My throat felt tight and parched from disuse.

An arm banded around my back and inched me slowly upwards. A hand was put to my dry lips and I was instructed to drink. I wrapped my lips around the heel of someone's hand and drank more than was possible. After I had my fill, I dipped my face in the little pool to bring life and lucidity further toward my senses. "W-What happened?"

I opened my eyes and saw Charles Mace, my newly discovered brother in front of me. His hand was wet from feeding the water to me using his many magics I still did not understand. His long fingers brushed the blonde hair from my face with tenderness that made me relax and Jens tense simultaneously.

"You laplanded with Jamie," Mace explained, his face etched with relief. "You've both been out for three days."

"What?"

The only voice I wanted to hear in that moment whispered in my ear, "Shh. You don't need to worry about anything right now. Just chill and let yourself wake up."

I was leaned up against his chest, and the comfort of that was indescribable. My eyes began to focus again, and I saw that we were in some sort of thatched-roof hut with a mud floor. Mid-afternoon light crept in through the half-open doorway. Other than the straw bed and a large steel basin bathtub, there was nothing else in the hut. "Are we in... Where is this? Haiti?" I guessed, moving my fingers around to build up my circulation.

Jens shook his head and inched me up further so I could breathe better. "Nope. Still in Undraland. We're in Nightdwarf territory. Most of their civilization is underground. They lent us this aboveground house until you and Jamie get better."

"Jamie?" I glanced down next to me and saw Jamie's motionless form. He had a bit of color back and was breathing steadily now, thank goodness. I buried my forehead in my palm to cover my shame. "Oh! I thought he was you! I kissed his neck. Now it's all awkward. Could we not tell him I did that?"

Jens chuckled, shaking my torso gently with the motion. "You don't have to worry. Your Tomten prince's still out. I know you dream about me constantly."

"Oh, shut up." I rolled my shoulders and finally had the wherewithal to sit up on my own. I looked down at my bare legs and grimaced. I was not dressed in my clothes, but in a bag-like itchy dress that fell to my shins. "Why am I always waking up in a dress?"

Jens grinned, rubbing circles in my back. "Don't worry. I had Tor clean you up and dress you while you were out. I know how smitten you are with Jamie, what with you kissing his neck and all, so we gave you matching outfits."

Sure enough, Jamie was wearing the exact same thing. I mean, exact same, only the fit was not as baggy on his larger build, and the dress barely fell to the knee on him.

"I sincerely hope you're joking," I grumbled.

"You know I am. Britt took care of you two and washed your clothes for you."

Jamie's dress was cut open at the chest, showcasing several bandages wrapped around his torso. Then it started coming back to me.

The bear.

No, not bear. A Werebear. Pesta's own creation of sending harvested evil souls back out into the world to do her bidding. She was tracking me, sending out souls to kill me, while the bodies those souls came from were checked out and pretty much lobotomized in her Land of Be. "Where you can just Be" was the slogan. The retired Undrans had their little lifetime siesta, meanwhile she broke her word by weaponizing the forfeited souls. She had been allowed to use only bears to experience the world she had been banned from. Now she migrated to using other animals – a fact the many magical kingdoms of this surreal world were as yet unable to accept. She had murdered my parents and taken my dad's bones to start a portal for humans, opening up another race to use for her own devices. She wanted me for the rake she guessed was passed down and still in my possession. She also wanted my bones to finish the human portal, so a new race would be open for her perusal. The rake was the only weapon that could be used to destroy her portals. That was our mission.

I rubbed my temples as the information overload sizzled in my brain. "Tor got through to the portal and destroyed it?"

"We never even got close," Jens replied, chagrinned. "Our injuries were because we were running invisible through a battlefield. It was too well-guarded."

"Did any of the Daydwarves see you?"

Jens shook his head. "I don't think so. We were welcomed here with open arms, so no. To them we're your entourage, accompanying the 'human female' Queen Lucy around to the different regions."

Mace spoke up. "They're throwing a big party tonight to honor you."

"Huh? Um, okay. That's awfully nice."

"Might be good if you could walk by then," Mace hinted. "How do you feel?"

"Like I've been hit with a ton of bricks. What happened to me? Did I get some weird leprechaun flu?"

Jens snorted. "Leprechauns. You and that imagination." Then he shifted awkwardly behind me. "How did you guys escape the Were?"

"Henry Mancini!" I exclaimed, whipping my head around to the door. "Where's my dog?"

"Foss has your wolf," Mace answered. "Did you know it's not a dog? Might not be the safest choice for a pet. Your Tom should know better."

"Shut up, Mace," Jens growled.

"Henry Mancini would never hurt me. He's okay though?"

Jens nodded. "What happened to the Were, Loos?"

Moisture welled up in my eyes before I could stop it. I pictured my hand clutching Jamie's machete, terrified at the notion of using it, but knowing it would be worse if I didn't. "He hurt Jamie, so I... stabbed the bear in the belly. Twice, I think, with Jamie's knife." I couldn't bring myself to look at the men; I was so ashamed. "The second time I didn't drive it d-deep enough, so Jamie helped me finish him off." At this, I broke down into quiet sobs. "I'm sorry! I'm so sorry! I didn't want to kill anybody!"

Jens patted my back and nodded gravely at Mace.

My brother kissed the top of my head and drew me to his chest, away from Jens. "There, there. It's what you were supposed to do. You're lucky you both survived."

"He hit Henry Mancini!" I wailed. "He attacked my dog

and Jamie! Peaceful resistance wasn't working!"

Jens got up abruptly and left the hut with no explanation, plunging me into guilt-ridden despair over killing a living being. Charles wrapped his arms tighter around me as I sobbed like a baby. "You can't peacefully resist a normal bear, much less a Were. Lucy, it's okay. You're safe."

"It's not okay! Killing is wrong! Martin Luther King would have found a way!"

I spent the next fifteen minutes crying on Mace's shoulder while he tried unsuccessfully to understand my grief.

When Jens returned, it was with a hard expression that I wanted to cower from as he towered over me. "Give us a minute, Mace," he ordered. There was no mistaking the sharpness in his command.

Charles released me, wiping the lines of tears from my cheeks before rising from the bed. "You'll be alright, *kära*."

Jens stiffened at this and stared Charles down as he exited the hut. When it was just the two of us and Jamie's unconscious body, he crossed his arms over his chest and puffed his breast out authoritatively. "I don't like him," he ruled.

I wiped the last tear away and scoffed. "You have a hard time getting along with people? I don't believe it." I shook my head and brought my knees to my chest on the bed so I could rest my head on them. "You don't have to like him. You're completely free to make things as difficult as you need to."

"You know that's not what this is about. He called you *kära!*"

"Do you hear yourself? So what? Foss calls me rat. *Kära* is a far sight better than Tor calling me human female all the time. Queen Lucy. Lady Kincaid. So what? Because Charles is nice to me, now he must be the devil? Be more obvious, why don't you." My hand rested on Jamie's shoulder, and I lowered my voice so as not to wake him.

"Obvious? Talk about what's right in front of your face. *Kära* is like 'hey baby' here. It's a lovey term of endearment for lovers in love, with the love stuff." Jens's cheeks were turning pink. He looked like just pushing out the word love was strangling him.

I shook my head. "Don't do this."

"What? Look out for you?"

My hands flew out and animated my frustration. "Don't make things difficult like this. Charles is my brother now. I actually have a chance at making a family for myself again. Don't be a baby and fill my head with semantics to try and drive a wedge between us. I don't need protection from my own blood!"

Jens was so aggravated that his pitch rose to get his point across with more passion. "He does the hug and lurk!"

"The what?"

"You know!" He mimed a hug with his shoulders hunched inward. "When he hugs you, he doesn't let go when a normal person would. He hugs, and then he lurks.

The hug and lurk. Come on! It's plain as day that he's in love with you."

"Well, maybe you should yell at me about it!" I shouted back. "I can't believe you're doing this! I finally get... and then you... and I don't care what you say! There's nothing wrong with Charles or the way he looks at me."

"Ah-ha!" Jens yelled, pointer finger raised in triumph. "I never said anything about the way he looks at you. You did notice something off about him. You just won't admit it because then I would be right! And we can't have that, can we?"

I threw my head back in exasperation. "Oh! You are so arrogant! The world doesn't revolve around whether or not you're right, Jens. Charles is perfectly fine. I'm lucky I get a chance to have a family again! And frankly, you don't get a say in this. Your job is to protect me, not swagger around like a jealous fool. Newsflash, you're not my boyfriend!"

He struggled with which angry words to spit out at me, his face shifting from pink to red.

I didn't want to hear it. I stood and stomped past him with my nose in the air.

"Lucy, wait! I'm not done talking to you."

"Oh, yes you are!" I marched out into the fresh sunlight, but I couldn't fully enjoy it because of stupid Jens. I didn't know where I was going with no shoes on, but one thing was certain, that hut was too crowded for the both of us.

2

SISTERLY BONDING

The world not on the mountain was very green. Rolling hills with tall trees dotted the landscape. There were clusters of homes, but not enough for a whole nation of people. Then I noticed the mouth of a tunnel. Over the arched circle-shaped entrance was a sign that read, "Blessed are those who enter the deep. Cursed are those who enter with ill intentions."

Yikes. All this talk of curses was worrisome, since curses actually meant something here. Poor Jamie up and attacks people when he sleepwalks all because of a curse.

I looked back at the hut that Jens still occupied and ruled it as a no-go zone for the time being. I continued on, looking for familiar faces amongst the dozens of ruddy ones scattered about, when I saw Britta running toward me from another hut. She was wearing a sort of kilt with knee socks and a flannel sash across her torso, brown braids flapping as she ran. "Lucy! Are you well?"

Good for her, holding back her real question of "How is Jamie".

"I'm fine, Britt. Jamie's still sleeping. Where is everyone? Where's Henry Mancini?"

"Foss gave your... your dog to Nik, who took him underground with the rest of them. They're practicing drinking for the feast tonight. It's being held to honor you, so I'm glad you're awake." She put her arm around my shoulders and corralled me toward her hut, which was closest. "I'm sure you don't know this, but your gown is completely transparent in the sunlight. It's an undergarment not meant for wearing by itself."

I cringed, covering my breasts. "Oh, great. I didn't realize. I just ran out of the hut as fast as I could. Your brother's in rare form today."

Britta led me to the hut she emerged from, introducing me to a Nightdwarf family who looked shocked to see me apparently in my underwear. "Don't mind us," Britta said to the woman of the house and her two red-faced, pudgy children that were about two feet tall apiece. The woman bowed to me, which stopped me short. I didn't know what to say to her, so I gave her a forced smile and let Britta lead me away.

This hut had a bedroom that Britta had been granted use of. She shut the door behind us and pulled a cherry and gold flannel-patterned gown off the hat rack while I stripped down behind the partition and washed myself in the steel basin.

"This is for you to wear," Britta informed me. "I'm sorry. I only just finished making it, and I didn't have time to put it in your hut yet. Do you need me to help you?"

"I think I can figure it out. And, wow. Thanks for making me a dress. I've never had one made just for me before." I looked at the complicated stitching and elaborate ball gown-style strapless dress. "You have my regular clothes, though, right?"

Britta nodded, straightening her hair in its two usual braids on either side of her head. "Your clothes are in your green pack." She paused, her tone coming out strained. "You and Jens had a fight already?"

"I know. He's being a real pain today. Picking on Charles isn't cool, and I told him exactly that. Why can't he just get along with him?"

Britta smiled with her gentle grace when I came out from behind the partition. "Oh, that's exquisite on you. Just how I pictured it. And Jens isn't prone to making friends easily. I do know he cares about you a great deal."

I tried to fasten the dress, but doing a corset from behind is confusing. I fumbled with the lacing. "Lucky me. That means I get yelled at five minutes after I wake up from the worst flu of my life. Do you know if there's anything to eat? I'm starving."

"May I?" Britta began lacing up the dress in the back for me. "Jens doesn't know how to be vulnerable. That's what makes him such a reliable guardian gnome. I'm sorry he's been coarse with you." She jerked me with surprising strength to get the corset tighter. "Hold on to the door," she suggested.

I grabbed the knob to steady myself against her tugs, holding my breath while she finished lacing up my dress and pinning up the bustle. When she was done, I looked down at myself in awe. "Whoa. I've never worn anything this sexy before." I stretched my arms over my head to make sure my breasts didn't pop out spontaneously. I never had reason to wear strapless floor-length gowns back home. I'd never been asked to a school dance, and generally covered myself up pretty appropriately. Plus, you know how I feel about dresses. This one, though… This one I liked. I actually felt like a woman in it. Beautiful, even. I'd never seen a flannel ball gown, and wouldn't have thought one could be so flattering, but there I stood, Lucy Kincaid in a pretty dress. And I wasn't cringing.

"Lucy, you look lovely," Britta marveled, her eyes wide at my display of visible cleavage.

"Do you think so?" I asked, my insecurity poking through. "I kinda like the dress. You really made this? You're incredible."

"It's absolutely breathtaking on you. Would you like me to do your hair?"

I nodded and sat on the bed while she twisted and fastened my blonde waves into a complicated updo with many braids and knots to make the hair match the dress in its elegance. "How did you do that?" I wondered aloud when she finished. "I could try to do your hair like this if you can talk me through it."

Britta blushed as if I'd asked her what her bra size was. "Oh, that's okay. I don't need to look impressive to the Nightdwarves. I'm not representing an entire kingdom."

I shrugged, my bare shoulders moving through the warm noontime air. I patted a spot on the bed in front of me. "Then look impressive for yourself. We can be matching. C'mon. I miss having a girlfriend." Britta complied with a gleeful grin, and I set to work.

There was no mirror, so I couldn't tell if our hair matched exactly, but she talked me through enough of it. When I finished, she looked more youthful and feminine than she usually did with her tightly wound braids and white Amish bonnet.

"Man, you're pretty. You should do your hair like this more often. Wait till Jamie gets a load of you."

Britta looked down at her hands in her lap. "Jamie's path is set for him."

My heart lurched in my chest for the poor girl doomed to love a man she could not have. I wrapped my arms around her from behind. "He hates his path, though. He's madly in love with you."

She leaned into me and spoke with great sadness. "I only hope the king doesn't find out. His father... King Johannes doesn't always have the best intentions for Jamie. It doesn't matter that he loves. His fate is sealed."

I kissed Britta's cheek. "Try not to think about all that right now. Today you're a woman with fancy hair and a new dress. Prince Jamie's in love with you, so enjoy making him work for it tonight."

She pressed her cheek to mine and giggled softly. "I'm sure I don't know what you mean."

"Oh, you're a minx, and you know it." We laughed together, sharing in the breath of fresh air the levity brought us.

"And what about you?" she asked as I pulled away.

"What about me?" I stood and straightened my dress, still enthralled with the gold thread and the dainty stitching. The bold pattern of the dress clashed with the elegance of the fit, making it my new favorite thing.

"Jens is going to have to work very hard to cause problems with you tonight."

I frowned. "Oh, I'm sure he'll find a way."

3

FOSS THE BOSS

*N*ik and Foss met us outside the hut Britta had slept in. There was no sign of Jens, and I couldn't decide if that was a good thing or a bad one.

The two men wore red kilts matching the pattern of the material of my dress and Britta's kilt. Nik escorted Britta. The poor girl was hit with story after story of wild boars he'd slaughtered in the name of border patrol.

You're amazing, Nik. We get it.

Foss offered his arm to me with great reluctance. "Let's get this over with."

"I can walk by myself. I wouldn't want you to be seen with a rat like me."

He scrutinized the sass I usually didn't bother him with. Whatever. I hadn't eaten in days. I didn't feel like pretending with him.

"The Nightdwarves think you have great value, so

you'll walk in with me. Your gnome's nowhere to be found, and my standing is higher than his, anyway."

"I'll do no such thing. I don't need someone who hates me putting on a show for strangers. Pass." I picked up my skirts and rustled past him. He moved in front of me, which only fueled my anger. I glared up at him, my scowl matching his. "You might be ashamed to have to work with me, but did it ever occur to you that I'm ashamed to be seen with you? You're horrible to me and Britta. I have a kingdom to represent. I won't be seen with your small brain and your bigoted attitude. Unless I need a jar opened, you're useless to me in this situation."

I saw Britta's head point down as she bit back her delight at Foss being put in his place.

Foss looked like, given the option, he would very much like to tear my head off. He certainly had the bulk to do it. "They need to see your kingdom's protected so they'll respect it. I'm the one for that."

I tried to don a more polite tone, since honesty wasn't getting me anywhere. "Thank you for the offer. Really, it's super nice of you, but I'm alright on my own."

Foss waited until Nik and Britta turned the corner ahead of us before he jerked me around, slamming me against wall in the mud hallway. His voice came out a forceful whisper. "You helped kill the Were, so I stand corrected. You're not completely useless. I've killed many, so I know it's no easy task."

I was shocked that he'd manhandle me so blatantly.

"Get away," I growled, slipping out from his grasp and shuffling down the hall in my swishy gown.

His palm found my back and pushed me roughly forward.

I tripped over my gold sandals and pitched down onto all fours. "Ow! Do you have to be so rough? Honestly!"

Foss yanked me up off the ground, which almost hurt more than falling had. "Do you have to be so clumsy? You're infuriating. I can't believe you're supposed to represent the best of your species." He gripped my arm and shook me as he spoke.

"You're hurting me!" I whimpered, fighting to extract myself from his control. "You would never pull a stunt like this in front of Alrik. Let go!" My pulse was racing when I finally wriggled out of his grip, rubbing the sore spot on my arm.

Foss cast around for Jens, scratching the horizontal line of tattoos on his forearm. "Have you really not seen your gnome? He can handle your mouth better than I can."

My arm was red, and my dress disheveled. "Jens was being extra charming last I saw him. I'm taking a breather so I don't get swept off my feet."

"Your problem is that no one's trained you. They let you do whatever you want in your world." Foss gripped my elbow in a way that chilled the blood in my veins. In that moment, I could tell he was capable of murdering more than just a bear.

He rammed my back against the wall again, one hand

pressing my shoulder into the mud-packed surface, and the other coiling around my throat. I thrashed in panic, but he was so much stronger. He pressed his body to mine, lowered his head and whispered through his teeth, "You may be the queen here, but wait until we get to my territory. We keep rats in their place there. Let's see how your pretty mouth fares with the Fossegrimens." He touched one of my curls. "They've never had a blonde to play with."

My heart thudded as I tried to struggle out of his grip, clawing at his meaty fingers. "Let me go!" I choked out. I built up a good scream, but Foss released my shoulder and covered my mouth with his massive mitt.

"Here's how this'll play out, rat. You'll walk in on my arm because that's how it's done here. You'll smile and be polite, follow the customs and impress the Nightdwarves with your ability to wear a dress. I'll act as your escort to show our kingdoms are united, and you'll say nothing about it. Nod if you understand."

I nodded, too afraid to cry. Despite the warmth of the day, my body was cold all over. The hairs on my arms stood to run from Foss. I felt disgusting and disgusted and very, very small. Oxygen was hard to come by as his grip tightened around my throat.

"Are you afraid?"

I nodded, fighting to suck down a portion of a breath, wishing more than ever for my dad to rescue me.

"Are you scared enough to obey without causing me any more trouble?"

I closed my eyes and nodded as the world grew a little foggy and my knees felt weak.

In the next second, Nik was on Foss, shoving him off of me. Foss released me, and I whimpered as I collapsed to the earthy ground, feeling my throat and hugging myself to shake off the grip of Foss in all of his violent swings.

"What are you thinking?" Nik shout-whispered, so as not to draw attention to the madness. Foss came back at him, but Nik surprisingly held his ground. "You could've killed her!"

"You can see she still breathes." Foss glanced over his shoulder toward Britta, who tucked the knife back into the pocket of her dress. She was fuming as she helped me to stand. Foss glowered. "She breathes, but now she won't speak out of turn."

"This is not the way. I told Alrik it was a mistake to bring a Fossegrimen on the journey. He'll hear about this, make no mistake."

"I don't fear Alrik," Foss lied, his bravado in full swing.

Nik scoffed. "Then you're a fool." He moved toward me, fingering my neck to check for damage. "Are you alright, Queen Lucy?"

I nodded, bottling up any tears that threatened to spill over. "I'm fine." I shrugged away from Nik and Britta, whose sweetness was a danger to my composure. I touched the heart that held my brother's ashes on a braided rope around my neck, hoping it would calm me.

Foss pushed Nik out of the way. "I can handle her. Be

on your way. We're already late, which doesn't bode well for her rule."

Nik made eye contact with me. "I'm just up here. Shout for me if he tries anything like that again."

"Okay." I knew if Foss tried anything like that again, he was likely to kill me. But sure, I'll try for a scream.

"I trust Jens walked you through what's expected of you?" Foss inquired, offering his arm like a command and a dare to disobey.

I took it, hating him and myself with every step we took. "No."

"Excellent," Foss grumbled. "If I were you, I'd request a transfer from King Johannes himself. Can't rely on a junkie to come through every time." He took a deep breath as we walked into the tunnel, encouraging me to do the same. I got the impression that as we moved forward, we were also going down further into the earth. The dirt walls and ceiling were lit with hanging jars that had glowing bugs inside them, casting shadows that made me jumpy in my already frightened state.

My arm was looped through his as he leaned low to talk to me on our walk. "Nightdwarves are much like Tor. They'll expect you to prove yourself somehow. They drink a lot of Gar, so be prepared to join them for as many shots as it takes."

"I don't have much experience with drinking."

I could tell this was the wrong thing to say by the silent alarm in his eyes. "I take back any mention of you being useful to us." He ran his hand down his face. "No time like the present to learn to down a shot. Try not to let the drink hit the front of your tongue. We can't have you blanching like a child and insult them." He thought further, scratching his short black hair. "Don't let them bully you. They only respond to strength, so don't let them talk for you or over you. You are the most important person they've ever met, as far as you're concerned. If you don't go into this like that, they'll walk all over you, and the human race will be the butt of jokes for centuries to come."

"What?" All of this was making me very nervous. The absence of Jens, an empty stomach and the beginnings of a headache in the back of my brain all made me want to run and hide. "Foss, there's no way I can walk into a roomful of Tors and make them think I'm amazing. I can't even get Tor to think I'm halfway useful! This is a bad plan!"

Foss stopped our progression and moved me over to the side of the tunnel, pressing my back to the packed dirt wall in the same manner, but less forcefully. Panic lit me from the inside once more.

Again, his hand covered my scream as I struggled between him and the wall for escape. "You'll do this because you must." His body squashed mine to the wall, and I only barely was able to fend off a panic attack.

"Let her go!" Nik sang in full operatic tune.

Just like that, Foss's arms dropped to the side. He shook his head, clearing it of Nik's enchantment that was delivered through song. "Don't try your Nøkken tricks on me."

Nik shoved Foss aside. "This is not the way, Foss! You cannot scare confidence into her." Nik's arms went around me to quell my trembling. "You listen to me, Lucy Kincaid. I've met exactly one human, and she can handle a lot more than you're giving her credit for. You knew nothing about any of this a month ago, and here you are, a queen amongst the common."

"But I…" My breathing was unsteady as the trepidation thrummed in my vessels.

Nik held up his hand to stave off my protests, posturing at the feel of a woman in his arms. "We're a team now. You and me and the rest of us famous outcasts." He cupped my chin and raised it so I was looking into his serious eyes, his white-blue hair sparkling as the bug lights illuminated him in parts. "Hold your head up high for all of us. Do you think Foss really killed hundreds of criminals? Do you think Jens is really worth all the hype? What about Jamie? Sure, he's got the title, but he's a leper in his own family. We're the elite, but we don't belong with our people. I want you to go in there and let them know you're worth the gossip. You belong anywhere you put yourself, because that's how amazing you are." He pointed further into the endless tunnel, whispering in my ear. "You own that ballroom. You own any room you walk into." He laced his fingers through mine and brought our joined fist up between us. "Make them beg for a look from you, the great Queen Lucy." He turned to Foss, giving him a shove. "And you'll protect her like a man, not abuse her like a beast.

This is not your kingdom. She'll not end up another mark on your arm." He pointed to the tattooed lines on Foss's forearm, and I watched as Foss clenched his fist.

Tor was running toward us from up ahead, beckoning us forward and scolding us for being so late. Nik kissed my knuckle, nodded once he was certain of my resolve and handed me to Foss, who led us down into the earth.

4

HEADACHES AND VOICES

I had gone to exactly four social parties in my life. One was an obligatory slumber party that every girl in the first grade class had been invited to. Rachel, the birthday girl, had gotten my name wrong. She called me Lacey all night, and until we moved a few months later, that was my name at school. The teacher even began referring to me by the name that was not mine. Two had been parties that Linus had been invited to through sports teams, and the last was one that Tonya took me to for a friend of hers that thought I was trying to steal her boyfriend, who I'm still not sure I ever met.

This was different.

The underground tunnel led to a massive dirt grand hall, bigger than two football fields and with grass ceilings so high, I was shocked that we'd gone so far underground. The notion of being spontaneously buried alive if an earthquake happened occurred to me, further impeding on the calm Foss tried to scare into me. In the four corners of the grand room sat four golden boar statues the size of a rhinoceros. They gave off a golden glow, illuminating the room along with the hanging lamps that had those lit-up bugs inside. They were the same as the golden boar I'd seen in the painting at the palace in Elvage, only these were motionless statues.

Foss held my hand that was wrapped around his arm and led me all the way up to a raised platform.

Tor bowed and introduced me, quieting the room of thousands to hushed whispers. "Mighty King Dane and Queen Lovisa, allow me ta intraduce ya ta Queen Lucy of the Other Side."

There was a grand table where two red-haired and red-faced dwarves with crowns greeted me with a skeptical eye. "Aye, human female," the king said by way of a hello. He was a whole inch taller than Tor, and I wondered if that was some sort of sign of being elite. He had a big bulbous nose with a giant mole on the side that I tried not to address directly when I spoke to him.

I dropped Foss's arm, raised my chin and stared him down with a cool calm covering over the fear that was coursing through my veins. "My friends call me Queen Lucy, not 'human female'."

The king's eyes widened at being corrected. "And yer enemies?"

I summoned every childhood movie I'd ever seen with

a wicked stepmother or an evil queen and said, "Dead men can call me whatever they like."

Suck on that.

The King of the Nightdwarves gave me an appraising look and then belted out an enormous belly laugh that made spittle fly out of his mouth and catch on his beard. His wife grinned with her freckled chubby cheeks and handed me a shot glass of... something. She also wore a cleavage-bearing flannel-patterned gown, and it looked super cool on someone even shorter than me.

King Dane raised his hand, and in an instant the thousands of dwarves in attendance scattered about the grand ballroom grew silent. He raised his shot glass in the air, and the crowd mimicked his motion. I followed suit, earning a nod of approval from Foss.

"Tonight we welcome Queen Lucy, friend of Torsten the Mighty. Our honored guest will know the real hospitality of the Nightdwarves." Then he raised his glass higher, and the crowd mirrored him.

In unison, the room proclaimed, "Tomorrow we fight, but tonight we drink!"

Glasses everywhere clinked, and the amber liquid was downed. The king turned to me, bashed his shot glass to mine and met my eye in a challenge.

Foss and Tor nodded, so I put all my focus into drinking whatever was in the glass. I'd seen enough westerns and 007 movies. The real men took their alcohol without a breath. They didn't grimace afterwards, and they didn't leave the glass half-empty. This was a rite of passage for these people, and I would treat it as such.

I tipped the glass to my lips and muscled through every instinct to gag or barf or wince. I kept my gaze steely as the fire ran through me, lighting my insides with what tasted like salad dressing mixed with jet fuel. I drank with thousands of beady eyes on me, judging my every move. I swallowed with vigor and slammed my shot glass to the table twice, hoping the international symbol of "another round, barkeep" was understood here.

It was vinegar. Gar was some homebrewed version of apple cider vinegar. My parents used to drink it, and I never understood why. I fought the urge to vomit. Luckily, my stomach was pretty empty.

The king gave me a rousing "hey-oh!" which the entire ballroom echoed with vast amounts of cheers and applause. "Join us at my table, Queen Lucy, and her friend, Torsten the Mighty. Foss, the four powers are always welcome in the mines."

Tor slapped me on the shoulder, relief plain on his face. As much as they all told me I'd be fine, I could tell he had been as anxious as I was to see how the masses accepted my performance. "Yer a golden one, Queen Lucy."

I raised my eyebrow. "Not 'human female'? Well, now it's out. You're in love with me. I should've guessed as much."

Tor grumbled in his usual way that I was beginning to find adorable. He took a seat next to the Nightdwarf Queen and began chatting animatedly with her. I could tell he was doing his best not to stare at her obvious breasts.

Foss pulled out an ornately carved wooden chair for me with garden gnomes etched into the legs. I tried to trust he would not pull it out from under me, but I braced myself just in case.

He sat in a larger chair built for esteemed Foss-sized guests next to me. He leaned down and whispered, sending a chill of fear up my spine. "Sit tight and try not to let anyone know you're about to be sloshed."

"I'm fine," I argued quietly, my temples pounding. Everything was so loud.

"When was the last time you ate?" he inquired.

"Don't pretend you care about me. You don't get to pick and choose when you're nice."

I looked around the grand hall and saw a table of tall outsiders toward the back of the room. I waved to Uncle Rick, Nik, Britta, Charles and Henry Mancini, who raised their glasses in toast to me. I turned to Foss, who was still sitting too close to me, making me jumpy. "Go sit with them."

He leaned over and spoke in my ear. I fought the urge to shove him. "I'm Jens for now. The Fossegrimens are sworn allies of the Nightdwarves. It looks good for me to be at your side. It's just fortunate timing that Jens decided to childishly ditch his responsibilities tonight. You may not have earned your throne here, but I have."

I frowned. "But when will you eat? I told the kitchen to poison your food so the female population can sleep at night. I'm kinda anxious to see which poison they use."

He had the nerve to chuckle. "Be grateful you get to eat dinner up here with me. You could be listening to stories about Nik's magic hair or his heroic fingernails."

"That's the weapon I plan on using next time I kill a Were."

Oo, too soon. I tried to make a joke of my horrible act, but I wasn't ready to laugh about it yet.

Foss rested his hand on my naked shoulder and squeezed.

My skin crawled as I shrugged away from his touch. "Is your headache going to be a problem?" he asked.

"How did you know?" I was grateful that the party was in full swing, and no one seemed to pay me much mind, now that I was declared a friend.

"You're laplanded. You're still in transition. It's normal."

"I have no idea what you're talking about. Is that the dwarf word for getting drunk? Because I'm not."

Foss chuckled. "Give it five minutes, featherweight." His tone switched to concern. "Didn't Jens explain to you the phases of the lapland transition?"

"I really have no idea what laplanding means. People keep saying it, but it's not a term humans know." My stomach growled. "Food is a word we're quite familiar with.   Stab-you-in-your-sleep-if-you-touch-me-again   is another."

Foss's lax hand on my shoulder gripped hard. "Please tell me this is one of your jokes no one understands but Jens. Did anyone explain to you what laplanding is?"

"What? What is it? I'm sure my headache will go away soon. And get the smack off me."

Foss swore and released my shoulder, looking toward the entrance for Jens, I assume. My international translator and personal aggravator.

I forgot about my confusion, though, when platters of food came out of the kitchen and landed on my table. I waited until Tor took his first bite, and then I tore into mine. I mean, obliterated it. A whole plate of meat, root vegetables, hard rolls and corn, gone in five minutes. I even beat Tor, who looked on my appetite with appreciation.

"You'll want ta go easy on yer second plate, yer majesty." Tor rolled his eyes at the formal address. "T'won't do ta have ya horking it back up in front of tha entire kingdom."

"That's cool. I'll just aim my chunks your way. You look real pretty, by the way." He'd greased his dreadlocks so they were a little more manageable. "I kinda want to Barbie your hair in some fancy do."

Tor murmured something surly, but I couldn't decipher it. My headache decided to take a turn for the worse and crank up a decibel. I winced and drank a mug of water, hoping it would do something to alleviate the tension in my temples.

Tor was busy chatting up the queen. I'd never seen him be so charming. He was grinning and laughing at every little quip she made. It was cute to watch him suck up to the royals. I made a mental note to tease him about it later.

My head was pounding to the point I could no longer ignore it. When the music started up and thousands of dwarves began dancing and shouting their joy, I bit my knuckle to keep from crying out in pain. There were flutes and big bass instruments being plucked in such rapid syncopated rhythms, that beneath my pain, I was amazed. The dwarves danced with abandon. They were jumping, clogging and twirling, looking like a sea of spinning red kilts.

Please, no. Say it's something else, Jens. Say it'll go away! A voice in my head that sounded like Jamie surfaced. My internal monologue normally sounded nothing like him, but I tried not to worry. I shook the crazy out of my head and grinned when I saw Charles making his way toward me.

"Would you care to dance with your old brother?" he asked, a twinkle in his strange eyes.

I rose from my chair. "Of course! Thanks for asking. Tor stopped being charming a while ago."

"I can imagine."

Foss stiffened, looking me over as I stood. "Don't go far. Stay in this area where I can see you."

"Don't tell me what to do," I grumbled.

Britta? Where's Britta?

I winced and moved back when Jamie's voice bombarded my head again.

Foss gripped my upper arms, pulled my body to bend toward him and spoke loudly in my face over the music. "Have the voices started?"

"What?" My smart reply caught in my throat. No matter what world we were in, I'm pretty sure hearing voices in your head was the international symbol for going crazy. "Of course not! Why would you ask me that?"

"The moment the voices start, you must tell me."

Fat chance. I won't be shoved in a loony bin after keeping my head through all this. I tried to use mind over matter to soothe my nerves.

I don't hear any voices. I'm just tired from that flu. I don't hear any voices. There is no spoon.

The problem with this is that my mind was apparently being infiltrated by a big batch of crazy. I heard Jamie again, shouting his fears. *I have to get to her! She has no idea what's happening to us!*

I put on a smile to cover over the terror and took Charles up on his offer to dance. He led me down the platform out onto the dirt floor where the thousands of Nightdwarves danced with all their might. I tried to mimic them, but it was so jubilant and erratic, it was hard to call it true style. Charles did a sort of tango with me that was done at a jumping trot. I tried not to lose my lunch or get too dizzy from my headache and the Gar that made my guts roil.

Oh! My stomach. How much did I throw up? I feel like I've been run over by a horse.

I tried to smile through Jamie's voice bombing my brain again. I lost my step and fumbled through the rest of the dance, taking my Gar-chugging victory in front of the people down a notch at my clumsiness.

"Are you well, Lucy?" Charles asked, slowing the dancing down a little to accommodate my gross ineptitude.

My hand went to my forehead. "I think I'm a little tired. When am I allowed to go lay down?"

"Anytime you like, *kära*. Foss and I can sneak you out of here."

"Thank goodness. Let's go now."

"I'm surprised you lasted this long. How's your headache?"

I gripped his hand as he led us toward the head table. "How does everyone know about my head?"

"It's normal when you're laplanded to get a good squeeze on your brain." He turned to look at me. "You look beautiful, by the way."

"Oh, thanks. Pretty dress, right? Britta made it."

"The dress. The woman. Jens is a fool to have missed this."

"Whatever. I needed a break from him anyway." I waved Foss over so he didn't have a conniption and attack me again. He'd been sitting at the edge of his seat and watching me like a sharpshooter. "I'm going to lie down for a minute. This headache's no joke." My temples were pounding in a rhythm separate from the banging at the base of my brain, and despite the dozens of lanterns beaming throughout the hall, my vision was starting to tunnel. I leaned on Mace's arm with too much weight to be casual.

"Hey, are you alright?" Charles wrapped an arm around my shoulders to steady me.

"I need to get out of here, like right now." My voice was shaking and the pressure in my brain was so intense, I feared moving my neck as we made our way up to the surface. When the next blast of Jamie's voice bombarded my thoughts, I stumbled backward into Foss.

My head! Ah! What I wouldn't give for some lavender powder. I know Jens has some. Where would he hide his stash?

I put my hands over my ears to stave off the voice, but it was coming from inside my brain. Clear as day, Jamie was in my head.

5

SCHIZOPHRENIA

As we walked into the daylight, my headache began to lessen ever so slightly. Charles motioned to the hut I'd woken up in, but I shook my head. "No. How about your place? Where are you staying?" I couldn't deal with a headache, voices in my head and Jens. Plus, I didn't think I could look Jamie in the eye with a straight face.

Charles kept his arm around my back and led me toward the hut he, Uncle Rick, Foss and Nik had been assigned respite in. "You'll feel better faster if you're with Jamie, but if you don't want to see certain people, I understand."

Foss opened the door to a one-bedroom thatched-roof hut similar to the one I'd been in with Jens and Jamie that morning. "Lay her down on the bed. I'll get her some water. Does Jens have any of his lavender powder? That might help."

Mace looked up at Foss and snarled, "My sister is not a junkie! You'll keep your poison away from her." He shut Foss out, led me to the bed and lifted my feet up. I pressed my knees to my chest in a hug meant to hold myself together, but when Charles covered me with a blanket and kissed my temple, tears welled in my eyes. It had been so long since someone had taken care of me in such a tender way.

Flashes of my mother tucking us in at night flooded through me. The memory of her love made me feel hollow, like my bones had little use or meaning. Like *I* had little use or meaning.

I can feel that! I heard Jamie say. *It's so strong!*

"Hey," Mace said in a soothing voice. "It'll pass. Your head will stop hurting in a little bit." His hand found my cheek and stroked my jaw. He started humming the same lullaby my mother sang to us every night before bed when we were kids.

"That's *Greensleeves*," I commented. "I didn't know you had the same songs here as we have on the Other Side."

Charles stopped short. "I never knew it had a name. Alrik hummed it to me when I was a child to calm me down."

I have to make an appearance, or it will get back to father that I slighted King Dane.

I wanted to scream. It sounded like Jamie was speaking into my ear, but he was nowhere to be seen.

Britta's going to love this kilt. If only this headache would pass!

"C-could I have a minute alone?" I asked quietly. I knew the tears were coming, and I didn't want a witness to my insanity.

"Of course. I'll be outside with Foss, in case you need anything."

"No, no. Go back to the party. I'm just going to take a little nap."

Charles left, and as soon as I heard him walk off, I slid off the mattress and looked for a hard surface. The walls and floor were packed mud and grass. The bed was stuffed with straw. There was a chamber pot, but I cast around for a better option to bludgeon myself with.

I would not be shipped off to a psychiatric ward in this world. If their medicine was anything like Jack the Ripper's day, I would sooner die than end up like that.

As I looked around for a better option than the toilet, the pounding in my head grew to an unbearable pitch. It was thrumming from the inside out, and there was so much pressure, I feared an aneurism. I had never experienced a migraine of this magnitude. I sat on the ground in my beautiful dress next to the steel tub used for bathing.

When the next unwelcome voice came, I was ready. Before Jamie could get out two words about his own headache, I bashed my forehead into the steel.

Peace.

That silence lasted an entire minute before the pressure increased again, and I heard my pain exclaimed via Jamie's voice in my head.

I gripped the side of the basin and really cracked myself on it this time.

I was rewarded with another minute of silence, too dazed to feel pain.

When the voice came back, it was shouting my name. I opened my teary eyes and found the hut was still empty.

It had finally happened. I'd gone crazy. I couldn't believe it'd taken this long.

I whispered a prayer for Linus to rescue me and slammed my forehead one more time into side of the bathtub.

Then I felt nothing. Blissful nothing. There was no pain. I heard no voices. I simply collapsed on the floor, eyes closed, and drifted off into my own personal Land of Be.

LAPLANDED

I opened my eyes too soon for my liking. Jens, Charles and Foss were shouting in my face and shaking my body in various places. The world swam, and I was lifted... somewhere by... someone. Truth be told, I was ambivalent about the fact that I was still alive. I was just grateful my headache was mostly gone, and the voice had stopped.

"He's coming out of it!" Britta called from across the room. "Jamie? Jamie, are you alright?"

I couldn't look at Jamie. I knew if I did, he would know how crazy I'd gone. Same went for Jens. And Charles. And heck, throw in Foss for good measure.

"Thank God, Loos!" Jens heaved his relief in my face, burying his nose in my cheek.

"Lucy, can you hear me?" one of them called.

I'm pretty sure I answered. Either way, my eyes were open. That should count for something.

"Do you know where you are?" Charles asked in earnest.

I grimaced and held my forehead. "Please stop shouting at me. My head's killing me."

Jens held my head in his hands and pushed down on the lump I'd given myself. "Well, yeah! When you knock yourself stupid, it's gonna hurt. What were you thinking?"

"It was an accident," I lied, sitting up and batting all the hands away from me.

"No, it wasn't," Jamie argued, rubbing a similar lump on his forehead.

My hackles rose at Jamie challenging my lie. "I'm not allowed to trip? I'm not allowed to be imperfect? Queen Lucy the Almighty Bringer of Perfection, right? What do you people want from me? I'm a checkout girl, not a queen!"

"I saw you do it," Jamie stated flatly.

"Did Mace do this to you?" Jens seethed.

Charles scoffed. "I'm standing right here, you know. I didn't bash my sister's head in."

"Why would you ask that?" I frowned. "Of course Charles would never attack me. I already told you what happened. Too much Gar. I tripped and fell and bonked my head on that tub."

"Give it up, little rat. Jamie can see everything. The

laplanding's complete." Foss crossed his beefy arms over his chest in his finite way.

My nose scrunched. "You know, I have no idea what that means, but I hate that you call me a rat. It's mean."

Jens buried his face in his hands. "I was going to explain it to you, but you stormed out when we got in that fight earlier today."

"How could you not tell her what's happening to her?" Charles was irate, his black brows furrowed as he glared at Jens. "This whole time, what must she have been thinking? No wonder she tried to knock herself out. She probably thought she was going mad!"

Jamie shook his head. "Guys, give us some space. I'd like a moment alone to talk to Lucy." When no one thought much of this idea, he shouted, "Now!"

For such a meek guy, I'd never seen a room clear out faster than when he ordered it so.

"Nicely done," I commended him. Just the two of us in the small house was more of a soothing balm than everyone crowding around and demanding answers.

"May I?" Jamie sat down at the foot of the bed I was propped up on and crossed one leg over the other, his hands folded atop his knee. "Lucy, there's something we need to talk about."

I had instant flashbacks of my parents gearing up to recap Uncle Rick's account of his rendition of the birds and the bees. I bit back a smile and prayed this would be a less horrendous experience.

"I'm very proud of the way you handled yourself with that Were. Jens told me about your bent against killing, so I can only imagine how hard that must've been for you."

"Thanks." I pulled the covers up over my chest, feeling a little exposed in the formal gown.

"You saved my life by picking up my weapon, and for that I'm forever in your debt."

My eyes were wide at his little speech. "Well, for what it's worth, you did most of the work."

He held up his finger. "About that. When I helped you drive in the machete the final time, we ended up killing the Were together. Something special happens when two people do that. They become laplanded." He took a breath and waited for my reaction.

"Um, cool?" I shrugged. "I got no clue what that means."

Jamie managed a wan smile. "It means that you and I are bonded for life. When two people become laplanded, it's painful to be apart, hence the headaches and the voices."

Goose bumps broke out on my arms and the air suddenly felt hard to suck down.

He tapped his temple. "When we're together, there're no headaches."

"I don't hear any voices," I lied, afraid to admit my insanity.

Jamie reached out and patted my hand. "I know how overwhelming this all must be for you. You know, Jens tells me your parents were laplanded. It's one of the reasons their marriage was so strong."

"Huh? My mom doesn't believe in killing. She was a vegetarian."

"What's a vegetarian?"

It was my turn to look at him like he came from another planet. "Someone who doesn't eat meat because they're morally opposed to the killing of animals."

Jamie was amused, as if I'd just said the most ridiculous thing to him. "Well, that's nice. No wonder you feel so strongly against violence."

I nodded, hugging my knees to my chest and pulling my skirts down over my toes under the blanket. What a waste of an awesome dress. "So we're tethered together? For how long?"

He swallowed, and his response came out almost inaudible. "For life."

My stomach churned. "What? No, no. No, no, no, no, no."

Jamie tried to hold my hand, but I gripped myself harder, sitting in a ball on the bed. "I know it's not ideal. If we're near each other, it's like nothing's changed at all. No headaches. And over time, I've heard the headaches from being apart get less and less. The tether gives you more slack as you learn to use it. Eventually we might be able to get a whole mile of space if we work on it."

"A mile? That's it? But I... I..." Flashes of my parents always getting jobs where they could work together hit me with their odd coincidence. I'd thought it was romantic how they couldn't bear to be apart. Waitress, cook. Receptionist, accountant. "How do we undo it?"

He shook his head, finally letting his defeat show. He didn't like this any more than I did. "It can't be undone. It's nature's response to us killing together. Now we'll always be together. There was a soul in that Were, so we killed some*one* together, not just a random bear."

Maybe one day I'd find comfort in all of this, but today it felt like a portable prison. "I... I need some air."

Before he could stop me, I was halfway to the door. I opened it to the early hours of the night and bolted forward in the red glow of the giant moon. I had no idea where I was going, but it didn't matter. I had to escape. I ignored the shouts of Jens and Charles as I ran, my dress impeding my quick escape.

Dread coursed through my veins when my head started to pound. I tried to muscle my way through the pain and keep going, but the tether snapped me like a rubber band. The pressure was so great out of nowhere that I fell to the ground on all fours, unable to open my eyes. I clawed at the grass, inching my way further from Jamie.

Ah! My head! Stop, Lucy! Stop!

I felt Jens pick me up and run me toward Jamie, who was also on the floor. Guilt nudged me when I realized that I'd done it to him. Jamie. I barely knew the guy, and now we'd never be rid of each other.

Jens brought me back inside the hut and flopped on the bed, pulling me to sit next to him. His arm wrapped around me in a hug that was meant to comfort him, not me. He let out a desperate noise of frustrated defeat into my hair. "I hoped it wasn't true. With everything in me, I wished it. Tried to grab onto any other possible explanation. No, Lucy!"

I held him, offering what comfort I could in my utterly flummoxed state. I was still trying to wrap my mind around what Jens had days to process. I shushed him, wrapping my arms around his neck and leaning my head on his shoulder.

"I waited so long for you to see me! I've been invisible in your life for five years! I finally get to be with you, and now you're linked to my best friend?" He shouted into my hair again and gripped me tight, his grief washing over me like a flood. "And the worst part is that I can't leave you! I have to watch while you and Jamie build a life together!"

Jamie picked himself up off the floor where the headache had knocked him, and knelt next to us at the side of the bed, hands clasped in supplication to his forehead. "I would never do anything to take her from you, Jens. I would never betray you like that. You're a brother to me, more so than my blood."

I could feel Jens's heart pounding as he gripped me. His hand cupped the back of my head, fingers digging into my scalp as he shook with anger at the lot we'd been dealt. He spoke to Jamie through gritted teeth. "Have you ever known a man and a woman who were laplanded that did not marry and have children together?"

"Stop it!" I yelled. "Don't talk like that! I'm twenty years old, Jens! I don't want my whole life planned out for me."

"But don't you see that it already is? How will you get married to some amazing guy and explain that Jamie comes with the package? And what about his betrothal? Do you really think Freya will be fine with a queen sleeping down the hall their whole lives?"

"The curse!" Jamie moaned. "What about the curse? It's not safe to be near me in the night. You know what I could do to her in my sleep!"

I gulped. "We can sleep in separate rooms, can't we?"

Jamie pressed his fists to his eyebrows in frustration. "I live alone because I'm a violent sleepwalker! I'm not safe to be around. My curse runs deep, Lucy!"

I shook my head, my heart reaching out beyond my own grief to his. I put my hand in Jamie's curly brown hair, glad that he'd forsaken the use of his small gnome hat back in Tonttu. "You've never attacked Britta or Jens."

"Because I love them!" He buried his face in the mattress. "I do not love you, Lucy. I'm sorry. I barely know you."

I took in Jamie on his knees and Jens in his besotted state at my side. Someone had to be the adult and pull us out of this mess rationally.

I counted to four, and when I spoke, my voice was devoid of the stress looming over the room. "It's fine. We'll figure this out." I tried to push past all my fears and questions and lead us to some sort of middle ground between acceptance and despair. I kissed Jens on the cheek and found that it was wet. "Jens," I cooed, stroking the short hairs at the nape of his neck. "It's okay."

"How can you say that? I've loved you for so long, Loos. You have no idea what it's like to be so head over heels and have the person not even know you're alive. Then I finally... and then this happens?" He looked at me as if it might be the last time his eyes got their fill of my face. "Now I have to watch my best friend live his life by your side? I have to guard your children? Watch while you fall in love?"

"Stop!" I shouted, hugging him tight, our hearts pounding against the other's. "Stop talking like I have no choice in my own life. I'm not marrying anyone, so don't go there in your mind. I don't love Jamie. No offense," I offered to the man on his knees who was tugging his hair in anguish. I pulled Jens's tattooed cheek toward me so I could whisper what I never meant to say to him so soon. "I love *you*, you idiot!"

Jens pulled back, his lips parted in awe. "You, what?"

I pressed my forehead to his. "Don't make me say it again. You know I do."

Jens kissed me, his eyes shut as if his heart was so full, he was in physical pain. He kissed my cheeks as he spoke, and I was very aware of the revealing nature of my dress.

"I've waited so long to hear you say that. To hear it like this?"

"You're really surprised I think you're an idiot?" I teased, trying to make this our moment. The two of us, not the three.

He let out a bitter laugh and buried his face in my neck. "I don't like the idea of someone knowing you better than I do."

Emotion was alive in me, despite my attempts at humor to push away the horror of the situation. It was a humbling thing to be loved by such a heroic man. To know he could have his pick of any number of adoring Tomten women, but chose me instead, warmed me to his affection all the more. But I'd murdered, and this was the price I would pay for the rest of my life. My heart panicked, but I remained on the bed next to him, determined not to run from him. From us. "Please don't give up on me. Not now," I whispered in desperation.

Jens nodded, my plea chasing away his fears for the time being. "Never." He kissed my eager lips. "You're right; we'll figure this out."

7

TORSTEN THE MIGHTY

*J*ens was too afraid for many reasons to leave me alone at night with Jamie, so I slept in my guardian gnome's arms while a mattress was brought in for Jamie to sleep on the floor. It was not ideal, but really, we were on a vigilante mission spanning mythological countries. None of our travel arrangements would be ideal.

Sometime in the middle of the night, I heard the rhythm of Jamie's heavy breathing stall. Then it picked up, taking on the cadence of an animal giving chase. My eyes opened, and I saw Jamie on all fours, growling and panting like a madman. I gasped at the drastic change, and the noise set him off. Jamie jumped to his feet and roared at me, lunging for my face as if he meant to tear it from my body.

"No!" I shouted. Before I could do anything else, Jens

was awake and wrestling Jamie on the floor. I moved to the furthest corner of the bed and pulled my knees to my chest to avoid being swept into the rumble. Though Jamie was determined in his haze to attack me, Jens was ready for the task of taming his best friend. In no time at all, Jens had Jamie in a sleeper hold on the ground. He reached for his hand and did that pinch and stroke three times before Jamie went limp in his arms.

"Did he get you?" Jens asked, trying to catch his breath as he stood, cracking his neck.

"Jens, I don't want to do this! Can you take me home? Can we be done with Undraland? Please?" I begged. Seeing the meek and kind Jamie try to tear my face off was too jarring to put in a neat little compartmentalized drawer.

Jens turned his back to me, and I could tell he was fiddling with the pouch at his neck. He inhaled something, and I watched his shoulders relax. "It's okay, baby. Just lay back down. Come on." He stepped over Jamie and pulled the covers out so I could get down inside them. He slid into the bed between Jamie and I. "He'll be fine for the rest of the night. Jamie's nothing to be scared of."

Despite his attempts to pacify me, I was shaking like a leaf under the covers as he drew me into his arms. His long body was strong, and I tried to draw comfort from the bulk. "I don't like this," I told him in a whisper.

"I know." He kissed my lips once and focused on

rubbing reassurance into my back with his thumb. "I'm here. Go to sleep. I've always kept you safe."

I clung to him, but it was at least another hour until either of us drifted off to sleep.

When the morning came, we all met in our hut, since it was the only one not being shared with a Nightdwarf family, but was reserved for guests of honor. Jamie could not look at me, and I couldn't blame him. I'd overheard a lot of his lusty musings concerning Britta during the night through our psychic connection after his attack, and I could tell he knew. It would be a long journey of finding our stride.

I set about making Britta my new best friend, which really wasn't much of a leap. We were dressed for the journey, my lovely gown packed away in Jens' magical bag that could probably fit a rhinoceros inside if that's what we wanted. Britta sat next to me on the bed, twisting my hair into several braids that were pinned up on my head so my long curls wouldn't be a hindrance. As Uncle Rick explained the plan, I did the same to her hair, loving that we matched.

Oh, her hair's so perfect when it's out of those braids. Mm, Britta. I wish I could throw away her bonnet so she'd have no choice but to show me that beautiful hair. Jamie's thoughts were sweet, and much more G-rated in the daytime. *Freya has the teeth of a horse, and hair to match.*

I coughed to cover my small laugh at Jamie's thoughts.

Uncle Rick continued talking to the group. "We

decided it would be best to let them think we've left their kingdom before striking down the portal. We'll team up with the Toms and hide on the outskirts of their land until dark. Then Tor will take the rake and destroy the portal, leaving the rake with Jens to bring to the next destination. This time we all stay together."

This seemed reasonable to everyone, so we packed our bags and said our goodbyes to King Dane and his queen. Tor, Foss, Jamie and I received special gifts from them, as well. I bowed to them as the queen placed a heavy necklace around my neck. "A token of our friendship to yer kind," she explained.

Ah, they're making allies with humankind with a necklace. I thanked them and looked down, unable to keep my eyes from bugging out. The gold necklace was encrusted with so many diamonds and opals, I could not count them all. And the size of the jewels? I felt like I might get mugged at any second. I itched to take it off, but knew that would be a slap in the face the Nightdwarves would never forgive.

Jamie and Foss each received a golden axe, and I couldn't decide if they were decorative or actually useful. Tor was given a new double-sided axe he couldn't take his eyes off of. The king and queen kissed both my cheeks, and then we parted ways. Uncle Rick was adamant that we be seen leaving in the opposite direction in which we were going to head that night. If they thought we were trekking back up the mountains we'd just come from, then when the Nøkken portal on the other side was destroyed, we would not be as suspect.

I walked with my arm looped through Jamie's as we made our way through the small aboveground village. I know we had to show them that our people were a united front, but I could feel Jens staring a hole through my back as I walked, and it made me jumpy. "Hey, Britta. How much do you think this necklace is worth?" I asked, bringing her to my other side. If I was going to be stuck with Jamie, then Britta was going to be stuck being my BFF, whether she felt like it or not. I wouldn't have another person's life be ruined by this whole laplanding mess. Britta deserved to be happy, and I wasn't going to screw that up for her.

The more Britta and I chatted on our way, the more animated she became. She smiled and didn't mind explaining things to me that everyone else already knew. Then it dawned on me: she didn't see me as competition because she did not see herself as a worthy competitor for Jamie's heart.

Pfft. When I got through with her, Jamie wouldn't know what hit him. There would be no more talk of the two of us falling in love. They would have each other because she would always be around me.

Checkmate.

It was already working. Jamie and Britta guessed at how many houses in Tonttu the necklace would buy, and spun off into a whole conversation about different areas that were best for mining or whatever. I stopped paying attention.

I looked over my shoulder and winked at Jens, who smirked at my cunning. I could see his relief that there might actually be a way to make our burgeoning relationship work.

Job one, done. Job two was a bit more complicated. Getting to the opposite border we wanted to go to, disappearing, helping Tor destroy the portal with the rake while the dwarves were still nursing their hangovers, and going across Nightdwarf territory incognito. Piece of cake.

Uncle Rick and Tor were just ahead of me, and I picked up bits of their quiet conversation over Jamie's veiled flirting with Britta.

Uncle Rick held tight to the mission as we waited out the sun. He didn't want us to attack the portal only minutes after leaving the Warf. "And whatever you do, don't go through to the Land of Be when you're destroying the portal. You'll forfeit your arm and your soul, and you'll be of no use to anyone then."

Tor nodded, hefting his pack up on his shoulder. "Yep. There's no chance of us looking fer our family inside?"

Uncle Rick's answer was firm with no room for confusion. "Not if you want to help us shut Pesta down for good. Their souls were separated from their bodies once they entered Be. Your family isn't who you remember anymore. Their bodies are merely shells now." He squinted into the distance. "I can't imagine a more tragic sight than one of yours existing as a shell. You're best when you're robust and full of the life you exude. Pesta did your family a great disservice, taking such hearty souls."

"Aye." Tor did not respond other than that, only kept moving forward. Nik clapped him on the shoulder in solidarity as we walked. I hoped that when it was my turn, it would be over quickly so I would not be tempted.

Uncle Rick pulled out a piece of parchment paper and a crude pencil, thrusting them toward me. "Darling, in your clearest handwriting, I need you to write something for me."

"Okay, sure." I took the paper and pressed it to my knee so I had some sort of a surface to scribble on. When he told me what to write, I raised an eyebrow at my uncle, but obeyed, signing my name to the bottom as instructed. I handed over the paper. "What's it for?" I asked. *You'll never find me* seemed like something that might stir up trouble.

Uncle Rick gave me an indulgent smile with his signature eye-twinkle. "A little gift for the Mouthpiece," he answered, putting the paper on the ground and sticking a rock atop it. "By leaving it on this side, but traveling on the rest of our journey in the opposite direction, we'll lead the Mouthpiece up the wrong mountain. I heard tell at your welcoming party that the Mouthpiece was coming to meet Queen Lucy for himself and offer a treaty of peace. We'll most likely be long gone before he reaches the Warf."

"Oh, good," I stated flatly.

Jamie called to Tor, "You know, Lucy's never heard of your heroics on the battlefield."

Tor grumbled. "She doesn't want ta hear about that."

I skipped up to his side in my blue Chuck and my black, loving the feel of my regular clothes. I threw my arms around Tor in a hug that was certain to annoy my favorite dwarf. "I heard King Dane call you Torsten the Flighty. How'd you manage that title? Is it because you're always losing your keys?"

"Little girl, tha things I've seen would make yer hair curl."

"Well, my hair's already curly, so it can't be that bad. Did you give the king a nice foot massage? Braid his hair for him? He sure seems taken with you." Henry Mancini yapped as he scampered along next to me.

Tor glared at me and shook his head. "I slaughtered three trolls single-handedly, I'll have ya know. I saved tha Daydwarves from an attack in their district years ago, and that united our tribes." He looked more surly than usual. "Ya do one decent thing, and they build ya a pedestal. King Dane woulda taken care of it 'ventually, but tha queen was aboveground in the fields when tha trolls came out. I stepped up, and that's how I got on Alrik's map."

Uncle Rick was grave, despite the levity I tried to bring. "I chose you all for your bravery, sure. But I also chose you because you lost a great deal of loved ones to Pesta, and yet you resisted her charms. Physical strength is always a necessity, but strength of character is of great import, as well." He continued walking, setting a brisk pace. "Torsten lost seven family members in one day to Pesta, yet he continues on."

"A warrior has no place in tha Land of Be. I won't leave my armor behind." Tor was extra grouchy to cover over being revered. It made me want to pinch his cheeks just to piss him off. He sniffed the air. "Something's not right. We should move quicker."

Foss looked over his shoulder and saw nothing unusual. Still, we quickened our pace. Instead of disappearing at the furthest hut from the main village, we ducked behind the nearest one. Jens pulled the rake out from his pack and handed it to Tor. The usual awe and scrutiny of the ordinary object was to be expected. Tor softening was not.

"Now listen ta me, ya lot. I've fought with a great many warriors for many a good cause. I count ya up there with the best of 'em, and this cause the highest importance." He nodded, facing us with the rake in his hand. "It's been an honor."

Tor said his goodbyes briefly to each of them while I hung back with Henry Mancini. Uncle Rick busied himself with what he called "the ultimate diversion" after he hugged the dwarf. Tor bid everyone farewell for their own sake, but deep down, he was like me. We didn't believe in goodbyes or dwelling on things that didn't need talking about.

We paired up with the three Tomten, each of them

taking two of us, with me holding Henry Mancini. Tor held up his hand. "Wait. It might be my last time out in tha sun fer a while, and I'd like ta walk with Jamie and Lucy, if that's alright."

We resituated with Jens walking behind us so he could keep an eye on me for the few steps we remained visible. I wondered if I would ever get used to people putting such a high premium on my life. I felt a tingle go up my arm and knew Jamie had made us disappear from sight as we stepped out from behind the hut.

"Now listen ta me, you two," Tor began, speaking lowly to Jamie and me in his usual gruff demeanor. "I've known two who've laplanded with someone they wasn't married ta, and they didn't end so well. One drove a spike through her temple, and tha other... Well, none of them ended in a way proper ta talk about in fronta ladies."

"I'm not getting married, Tor," I said with absolution. "Not to Jamie or anybody. Now that I know I'm not insane, I won't give myself a concussion anymore."

Tor looked past Jamie to me. "Yer still a child. Ya don't know how yer life's going ta end up. But one thing's sure, if ya go off on yer own again, banging your head or trying to end yerself in some foolish way, you'll end Jamie, too. His death'll be on yer head. A human killing a Tomten prince? That's grounds fer war if I ever heard it."

A lump formed in my throat as the urge to run jumped up and choked me. The desire to wake up from this never-ending bad dream was palpable. Jamie squeezed my hand, but I felt nothing. As it was when confronted with a failed life plan, I was hollow inside. A smile with no substance. A body with no bones.

I hugged Henry Mancini to my chest, hoping he could find me in my black hole. "I'll be careful."

"Yer whole life? I've known ya for a coupla weeks, and I've not known ya ta be a careful one who values yer own neck."

"Which is it? You want me to be careful, or be like you?"

Tor growled at me. "Yer one insufferable female, Lucy Kincaid. Heaven help tha men stuck with ya."

I cast around for some end to his lecture. "What do you want from me? We can't all be Torsten the Mighty. Some of us are just trying to make it through."

"What's tha point in that?"

"It's done. We laplanded. I'm dealing. Jamie's dealing. You can back off. I'll make sure Jamie's safe. He can marry whoever he likes and I'll hole up in the attic. I can't imagine how any of this concerns you."

"You, Lucy. Yer my concern. Ya have ta do better than survive. Ya have to live!" Still holding tight to Jamie's hand and the rake, Tor kept his eyes on the portal we were approaching. "When all this is done, ya'll come see me and drive me mad some more, ya hear?"

"Only if I can shave your dreads off."

Tor squinted at me to make sure I was kidding. I was not.

He stopped and sniffed the air again, his posture stiffening when we were just a few meters from the portal, which was unguarded. With Jamie holding our hands, he turned and faced us. "Something's off. Keep yer hand tight ta me while I do this, Jamie."

Jamie nodded, sliding his hand to Tor's shoulder so the dwarf could have full use of his arms as he aimed the rake at the portal framed in dwarf bones.

The shorter skeletons stared at me with their black eye cavities and torn open jaws. Femurs and forearms were stacked end-to-end several inches wide to give the structure a bit of substance. I blanched at the macabre sight, my skin crawling to run away, lest the bones somehow animate and chase me around while I scream like a crazy person.

Then I heard it. A series of snorts closed in around us while Henry Mancini snarled in my arm.

8

THE PRICE FOR JAMIE'S VALIANCE

"It's the gullin and the Mouthpiece," Jamie breathed. "Try not to make a sound."

I obeyed, remaining completely motionless while we stared intently at the portal. The open doorway gave off a faint blue glow with an opaque sheen to it, casting rainbows and holograms on the grass. The passageway was framed with bones. Shorter than human bones and fatter. The frame was solid and thick, and I wondered how many dwarves had been sacrificed to construct it. I counted nine femurs.

Tor the Mighty raised the rake like an axe and blasted the left side, dislodging and scattering a whole mess of bones.

Then it happened. The blue light mutated, and red light shot out of the glassy doorway. Tor swung again, toppling the bones on the right side in one fell swoop, ending the portal for the dwarves.

Jamie gripped us both and bolted for the mountain, running just slow enough for Tor and me to barely keep up with our much shorter legs.

From out of nowhere (I mean, I know they came from somewhere, but they were behind me, so I couldn't see where they burst out from), golden boars the size of a car charged for the broken portal, snorting malevolently. They were the same ones that lit the ballroom, only they hadn't been statues; they were animated and terrifying.

I bit back a scream and ran my heart out, certain the organ was audible as it banged around in my chest.

Henry Mancini's bark was to be expected, but I cringed at the location giveaway.

"There!" cried a man who looked like he belonged to Foss's country. He was dark-skinned, tall and built like a WWE wrestler. His wild eyes and furious scowl aimed themselves in our direction. "Attack for your freedom!" the man yelled to the dwarf soldiers. I guessed correctly that he was the Mouthpiece, a body offered up by its owner for Pesta's indwelling.

Good choice. I mean, if I could be in anyone's body, I'd probably choose the biggest and baddest, too.

Several dozen dwarves in armor turned in our direction and let out a series of commands. The boars charged us, and I knew there was no hope. I wanted to tell Jamie to just go on without me, but what little sense I still possessed reminded me that if I was torn to bits, Jamie was a dead man, too.

I knew nothing about boars of this magnitude. Even if we made it to the mountain, which was half a mile away still, could they scale it?

Before I could reason this out, a loud explosion blasted from the direction in which we'd come. Then a second one boomed to our left. Henry Mancini barked and cried in my grip while Jamie charged faster yet. I felt a swoosh of wind tear past us, and then heard one of the boars squeal like a piglet in pain. There was a thud on the grass, and then another. I dared not look back, but I no longer felt them bearing down on us.

We ran until we reached the mountain, but the path was a ways to our right. Instead of running toward it, Jamie hefted me up over his head to a small outpost and did the same to Tor. "Get behind that rock!" he ordered. The second he let go of Tor and me, we were visible to the world. Henry Mancini and I scrambled behind the rock next to Tor, who was piqued with adrenaline. "That was Jens," Jamie breathed, invisible to my eyes. "He's out there fighting off the gullin, but he can't take on that many by himself and still get out of there. I need to help him."

"Then go!" I urged.

"It's going to hurt us, but I'll try to get him out quickly."

"Go!" I shouted, preparing for the worst. I hugged Henry Mancini, who licked my face over and over as I attempted to clear my mind. I knew that the further away we got from each other, our heads would start aching. Jamie needed to concentrate, so I did my best to meditate and think of nothing, so as not to add my errant thoughts to his workload.

Yeah, like that was possible.

The headache began at the base of my skull and slowly crept around my cranium until the whole thing throbbed like a vice around my temples. "Yer okay, yer okay," Tor said, patting my shoulder as I tried not to whimper. I lay down and spooned Henry Mancini so neither of us fell off the four-meter-high precipice. Tor muttered over and over in fearful and reverent tones about the bad omen it was that the Mouthpiece was set against us so soon in our quest.

Jens would be fine. He was built for this kind of thing. Jamie would be back in a minute. What was one minute of your head hurting?

Jamie's thoughts banged around in my brain as if they were my own. *Stop being foolish, Jens! Run! Ah!*

Pain out of nowhere ripped into my arm. I watched in terror as blood spontaneously began spurting out of my freshly ripped flesh. Tor cried out in surprise, snatching up my arm to examine the gouge. Ribbons of red streaked down my elbow and pooled on the rock.

"Keep calm, Lucy. The more ya panic, the more Jamie can feel that. He needs ta focus on getting Jens outta there."

I tried to keep my thoughts of alarm muted so as not to distract Jamie, but the combination of fear and pain was impossible to avoid. I cowered with my dog on the rock while Tor watched over me, waiting for other body parts to spontaneously start gushing blood.

9

THROUGH JAMIE'S EYES

It was near impossible to keep my mind blank, but Tor coached me as best he could. My head felt like it was being squeezed in a vice, my arm was bleeding, and my opposite hand had a scratch that was burning. It wasn't so much the injuries, but the threat of whatever might come next that made me jumpy.

"Just breathe, Lucy. Clear out yer mind and see if ya can look through Jamie's eyes."

I breathed through the pain and wished for my green bag that was crammed inside of Jens's red backpack. There was stuff to patch me up in it, but until I had it in my possession, I got to watch myself bleed all over the place. I tried not to look as I turned to my dual-powered brain and listened for signs that they were okay.

Arrows were flying across the battlefield from an invisible source, which I'm guessing was Britta. She sunk one deep into a golden boar that was gunning for Jamie, and I could hear his relief mingled with fear that Britta might be found out.

Jamie was yelling in his mind, which was not a good sign. I could hear him calculating an aim and then lunging. The breath was knocked out of both of us, but luckily he hit his mark with enough force to give us a few seconds to recoup.

"Look through his eyes, female!" Tor commanded.

"I'm doing the best I can!" I shouted, angry at his high expectations when I was clearly in peril. There was no learning curve in Undraland.

As I lay on the rocky platform cuddling Henry Mancini while he licked my wounds, I closed my eyes and tried to find Jamie. I focused all my energy not on hearing Jamie, but on seeing through his eyes. I wished and willed and erased myself until the world as I saw it faded in the center, and was filled by the face of a giant golden boar. Jamie stabbed into its neck, and the vivid imagery was like a kick in the face.

Focus! I told us both. He concentrated on the boar he was currently wrestling while I used my unique psychic viewpoint to look around the field. I counted seven dead sedan-sized animals with matted golden hair that glistened like glittered bronze in the evening sun. There were two dozen or so Nightdwarves in fighting gear, searching for the invisible foes that were tearing apart their defense line.

My eyes were cataloging things through Jamie that he could not, being so focused on the eminent danger as he was. I bit my lip to keep from screaming aloud when I looked to the left and saw the Mouthpiece taking aim at us. As loud as I could, I mentally shouted to Jamie, *Get down!*

An arrow whizzed overhead, and I was grateful that Jamie obeyed.

Good. We were becoming a team and learning to work together.

I kept sharp while I tried to ignore the pounding in my head and my various other injuries. Jamie fought with valor, and I was impressed with his heroic athleticism the entire time.

Another explosion boomed across the field. I looked through Jamie's eyes and saw fireworks blasting in the daylight. Not as amazing an effect as it would've been at night, but apparently no one here had ever seen fireworks before. The dwarves and Jamie fell back, and I could feel Jamie's fright. The boars forsook their prey and charged for the source of the blast.

It's okay, I assured the frightened Jamie. *I bet they're Uncle Rick's. They're fireworks. From my world. Totally harmless from this distance. Take your advantage, get Jens and get out of there!* When he did not move fast enough for my liking, I shouted, *Run!*

Jamie located Jens by a patch of blood on the grassy knoll a little ways off. My mind's eye saw him yank up the invisible man. I gusted out my relief when the two of them ran to the mountains. Toward me.

"They're okay! They're coming," I informed Tor, who was holding me tighter than could be comforting. The tension in my head slowly began to alleviate with every step they took toward us.

"Good girl! Ya did it!"

I collapsed with a gust of tension release on the rock while Henry Mancini whined for my attention. I gave him one pat, and then shut my eyes while I waited for them to find us.

10

STUCK TOGETHER

"Lucy!" came the whisper from just below my small hiding space. The sun was dipping below the horizon, and I felt the weight of sleep-deprivation, thanks mostly to Jamie scaring the smack out of me with his Jekyll and Hyde nonsense in the night.

I lifted my head and realized it was no longer pounding. "Jamie?"

"Yeah. Look, I've got to get you down so we can catch up with the others. Are you okay?"

I wanted to cry at the sight of him. Tor was climbing down on his own. "Yeah. I'm fine. Let me hand you Henry Mancini first." I lowered my puppy a few feet to the invisible man, grateful when he was gently taken from my hands without a struggle.

"Okay, just jump. I'll catch you."

I whisper-yelled at him, afraid to break the quiet that

was falling over the early night. "Are you kidding me right now? I know your arm's torn up. There's no way you can catch me! Mine's barely usable."

His answer was remorseful. "Oh, Lucy! I'm sorry! And I knew, I just forgot in the heat of battle. Laplanding's not exactly a common thing. Are you okay?"

"I'm exactly as okay as you are, minus the freak-out I've got going on up here. I'm fine, but I'm not jumping on you in your condition. Move back." I peeked around the rock and saw that the dwarves and boars were a long way off, running in the opposite direction. If I was quick, no one would see me. I turned around and lowered my feet from the platform, my fear of heights pinging my confidence, but not crippling it. If I fell, on the other hand, an actual crippling would be something to be dealt with. I froze for a second, the fear gripping my knuckles and shaking their hold on the rock. I really hated heights and the whole falling from them thing.

I breathed anew when Jamie's bloody but strong hands wrapped around my hips and lowered me gently to the ground. He scooped Henry Mancini back up and held my hand with his scraped one, ensuring that we were both invisible. Tor gripped Jamie's elbow to remain hidden from the enemy.

"Are you alright?" Jamie inquired.

I gave him a look to let him know he'd just asked me that. "How about you stop asking me, so I won't have to lie to you." My hands were shaking from adrenaline and the pain from my open injuries. "Let's find the others. Jens?"

Jamie nodded, still struggling to keep himself steady. "He's okay. I sent him further up the mountain path with Alrik and all them. A little banged up, but that's nothing. He's a better fighter than I."

"Let's go," Tor insisted, starting us toward our destination.

Jamie held tight to my hand, his nerves making him squeeze my fingers tighter than was comfortable. I stroked his arm to calm him down. "I saw you fighting, Jamie. You were heroic."

Jamie motioned to the path that was a few feet ahead. "The others aren't far. Let's sit for a minute. I need to clear something up." He turned. "Tor, can you duck along the brush until you reach the bend? I need to speak with Lucy."

"Be quick." Tor took Henry Mancini to the others, crouching the whole way and looking, well, kinda comical.

I scrutinized the horizon to be certain we had a wide margin of escape. The enemy was set on pursuing away from us, getting smaller by the minute across the stadium-sized field with a pile of bones from the torn-down portal in the center. I slumped to the ground next to Jamie, holding him upright as he sagged against the mountain and me. "What's up?"

"I don't want to get married either." His brown curly hair was windswept with splashes of blood in it. He was sweaty and cut and looked like he needed a good nap. "You told Tor you didn't want to marry. I understand. It's nothing to do with you. You're lovely. Absolutely everything Jens said you would be. For a while I was certain he was exaggerating your beauty and strength, but he was not. Even so…"

"You're in love with Britta." Before he could confirm or deny, I rushed to say my piece. "That's good! I like Britta. If we're stuck together, I don't mind spending lots of time with her. She's great."

He smiled in that patronizing way adults did when I talked about Martin Luther King's ideals. "If only the world existed as you see it. I do love her, yes." He let out a nervous cheer for his bravery. "I never permit myself to say it out loud, but I do. I'm promised to Freya, though."

"I've been thinking about that," I said, not wanting to hear his millions of ways things with Britta couldn't work. "I can fix it, I think. But we've got to get to the others. I know I look awesome, but if one of those rhinoceroses comes this way, I'm useless."

"Gullin are wild boars that belong to the Nightdwarves. They actually glow underground so to be used as a light for them when needed. Not rhinoceros. Boar."

I laughed at his explanation. "Really? You don't say. Come on, Hercules. Up you get." I stood and extended my less banged up arm to him and hoisted him up.

We walked, leaning on each other like coherent zombies until we reached their camp higher up on the mountain, out of visibility of the Nightdwarves and their pack of yellow rhinoceroses. I tugged on Jamie's shirtsleeve and placed my finger to my lips. I wanted to see them interact without us for a moment. I knew better than to sneak up on someone with an axe. I just wanted to watch Jens as he'd watched me for so long.

Jamie observed me staring at Jens for two whole minutes before he turned his attention to Britta. The group was discussing what they should do if we did not turn up shortly. Jens was in the conversation, but not. He was on the outskirts of the cluster, looking right past us for me. Anxiety was clear on his face. The emotion welled up in me, seeing how much he cared. Of course, I knew I was his job, but I could see with my own eyes it was more than that. He was pacing as he half-listened to the others.

Henry Mancini finally gave us away. Jens scooped him up and whipped his head around to find us. "Jamie?"

Jamie dropped my hand with a triumphant grin. "You look so worried, brother. I had no idea you cared so much for my well-being."

Jens gripped the back of Jamie's neck and they did that two-kiss Italian brother thing I really loved. Then his eyes fell on me. "Lucy! What have you done?" He picked up my bloody arm while Britta fretted over Jamie's identical wounds.

"Seriously? What have I done? I sat still and waited for you to come back in one piece. That's what I did. Thank your bestie here for running after you to save your tail."

Jens looked from me to Jamie and back again several times before it all sunk in. "Never again, Jamie! I didn't need you to sacrifice yourself like that. I was fine out there." His voice broke the reunion by turning sharp as he shouted as his best friend. "You can't ever do anything like that again! Do you understand me? You could've gotten yourself killed!"

Jamie postured. "I fared just fine out there by your side. My title does not make me useless."

"You can't play fast and loose with your life anymore! You're done fighting forever, you hear? You picked up your last sword!"

"Hey," I chimed in, placing my hand on Jens's tattooed cheek to bring him back to earth. "Calm it down. Take a breath before you say something you'll regret. Jamie's fine. He went out there to save you. I think what you're searching for is 'thank you'."

Jens spoke through gritted teeth. "I'll thank you not to put yourself or anyone else at risk. You take a hit, and she bleeds too! Did you think of that? What if you'd died? What then? I just lose both of you? Think, Jamie!"

Jamie pushed past Jens and moved to Uncle Rick so the elf could take a look at his wounds. Jens scooped up my bloody arm and dabbed at it with a rag from his pack that he wetted with water from his canteen.

"Jens, are you in there?" I asked, trying to look into the eyes that were avoiding mine. "Hey, buddy." I dragged my fingers through his messy black hair.

He batted my hand away in anger. "Don't you dare make light of this. You have no idea how bad this could've gone."

I wanted to argue, but sensed this was not the time. Instead I kissed the forehead that was bent over me, examining my injuries. "I love you, too."

He paused his negativity and wrapped me in a crushing bear hug. "Loving you sucks so bad, because this kind of thing happens! It would be so much easier if I didn't care at all."

"Sure, but then you wouldn't get these." I leaned up and kissed his stiff lips, knowing I'd won when they became malleable.

"Don't think Jamie's off the hook for this just because you work your magic on me."

I kissed him again, slowly savoring each movement that brought our passion to the surface. "Sure he is. My Kung-Fu is strong."

A hint of a smirk touched his full lips. "Alright, Jackie Chan. Let me wrap this up so Henry Mancini's friends don't smell you a mile away."

11

STRIPPING FOSS

Jens and Jamie were still not speaking after an entire night and then a whole day of trudging along on our mountain trek toward Nøkken. The sun was just dipping down, and we were all a little the worse for wear. My whole body hurt from not sleeping and from Jamie's bout with the gullin. I kept a pleasant expression in place, though. Anytime I made any noise of discomfort, Jens barked his anger at Jamie. I was getting good at being quiet.

Britta had gone up ahead of the group to try to find some food for us. I couldn't imagine what berries could be found on the sparsely greened mountainside. Everything was gray and brown, except for the occasional non-fruit bearing bush.

Foss turned abruptly from his spot ahead of me with a gruff expression that I was beginning to realize was his only expression. "We're not making good time. It's you," he accused, pointing a stabby finger toward me. "You're moving too slow. You'll get us all killed if you keep lagging behind like that."

I wanted to put him in his place, but I recalled my favorite historical figure's kind demeanor and donned a brave smile. "Sorry about that. I'll try harder."

The lack of a fight only made Foss angrier. "I don't know why you expect us to just wait around for you. It's you the Mouthpiece is after. I say we tie you to a rock if you fall behind again. Let Pesta find you so we can get some actual work done."

Jens shoved Foss, but the effort wasn't what I would've thought an indignant boyfriend would do. "Lay off, Foss. She's not your slave."

Uncle Rick stopped the progression, stomping his foot twice on the uneven path. "I think now is a good time to set up camp for the night. Charles, it's time for your lessons."

Mace's head bobbed in Uncle Rick's direction. He left my side for the first time that day and went to his adopted father. "You wish me to practice wind?" he asked, hands poised against the mild elements.

Uncle Rick motioned me over and spoke to me in a voice that carried to everyone. "Charles is the best and brightest. When they wouldn't allow him to attend school because of his bloodline, I took it upon myself to train him at home. Charles can manipulate wind if there is wind to speak of, and he can multiply and divide water if there is enough of a source nearby to draw from." His eyes twinkled at me, and I could see the pride he had in the boy so many cast aside as useless. "When your mother and father left him with me, he was fitted for a collar that kept him from whistling. It was precautionary. Just to make the public feel safe, really. Only Huldra women can control people with their whistle. The men have no extraordinary abilities." He stroked the side of his gray beard, and I could tell he had more beneath the surface of this story. Everyone else was listening in. "I've never been one for limits. People put too much stock in them. If you're cursed, you're always under the curse. If you're half-breed, you must not have enough magic in you to get out of bed in the morning. Undrans in general put too much stock in race and birthright, and not enough in study."

I produced a sleepy smile. "But you're not most men."

"Neither is my boy." He looked to Charles with sheer adoration. It did my heart good to know my brother had grown up with love. Uncle Rick leaned against the mountain and pointed at the surly mug that never cracked a smile. I wondered what Foss would look like if he grinned. "Charles, will you refill the canteens so Lucy can watch?"

Charles had the bashful grin one got when put on the spot doing a talent you were well-versed in. He picked up Jamie's canteen, showed me its almost empty contents, and placed his hand over the mouth. A few seconds later, I heard a steady flow of water, as if from a tap. He took his hand away and showed me the filled canteen.

"Whoa! Seriously? That's incredible!"

Charles's cheeks turned pink as he handed the canteen back to Jamie. "It fares well for me that you're so impressed with average elfin skill."

I turned my head to Uncle Rick. "You can do that, too?"

"Indeed, I can. But we can only manipulate water when there's a source to draw from. Had the canteen been bone dry, it would have been a disappointing parlor trick." He clicked his fingers with his palm facing the sky, and water began pooling in his hand and dripping through his fingers. He kept speaking as I watched in awe. "Foss's people were cursed when Pesta was sequestered to the Land of Be. It was a Fossegrimen who captured her and put her there, so the whole people bear a curse from her."

I eyed Foss, who snarled at having his junk spilled out for me to examine. "What's the curse?"

"Excellent question, dear. The curse was handmade by Pesta, and she named it The Depravity of Man. The Fossegrimen males don't have the same conscience we do. They follow their depraved instincts much easier than we would. Hence, the Isle of Fossegrim is bursting with rapists, slave traders, violent men and thievery." He paused to let that bomb sink in. "The more powerful the man was at the time the curse was made, the worse his curse. It turned Fossegrim from a thriving fish trade port to a den of horrors." He motioned to Foss with his staff. "Now our Foss started out his life as a slave, so the curse isn't as bad in him as it would be in two of the other powers that rule the island. I believe the chief also escaped the brunt of the curse, since he was merely a soldier at the time. Foss worked his way up and became the fourth power, using his cunning and depraved methods to get to where he is today. Foss is the fourth most powerful man in all of Fossegrim."

I suppose I should've been impressed, but my skin was crawling with the descriptions of the men Foss lived near. "So I should cut him some slack?" I inquired.

"On the contrary. That's all Undrans do is look the other way when a Fossegrimen pillages or a war breaks out on the island. We must teach Foss how to rise above his curse, otherwise we are telling him that he is weaker than his circumstance, a mere victim." He smiled at the fuming Foss. "And I know him to have strength to rival anyone on the isle."

There was a moment of quiet where everyone let Uncle Rick's words sink in. Then Uncle Rick tapped his fingers to the side of the mountain three times. "Charles, it's time for your lessons."

"Yes, sir." Charles stretched out his back, making sure to pay attention and show his father his due respect.

"You demonstrated that male Huldras have worth and can wield the whistle if they work hard enough. You've studied the whistle and its various components your entire life, as opposed to other Huldra men who dismiss the gift as inapplicable to them." He smiled at his son and motioned to Foss. "Foss is buried under layers upon layers of Pesta's curse. I put it to you to peel back the layers, one by one."

Foss backed up, wary of becoming the lab rat. "You'll not experiment with your illegal gift on me, half-breed."

Mace's eyes were wide, unsure of himself now that he was put on the spot. "Alrik, I don't know about this. I mean, fixing Lucy's eyes was an easy one. A siren's curse? A skilled female Huldra wouldn't be able to accomplish that! And I am not skilled."

Tor rolled his eyes. "Though he whines like a female."

I responded with a silent glower. Britta and I had barely spoken the whole day, and yet because we had ovaries, we were written off as weaker. She was off gathering food for everyone, and Tor had the nerve to cut us down.

Tor directed his words at Mace. "If Alrik says ya can do it, then ya have ta! Give it a try, halfy. Prove yer worth." He shrugged. "The worst you'll do is off this one, and I don't think anyone'd cry much."

Foss grumbled at Tor, but braced himself against Charles. "I don't need fixing, Alrik."

Uncle Rick stood, and even though Foss was taller, Uncle Rick seemed to tower over him in his kind, yet forceful manner. In a voice that demanded attention and obedience, he said, "Yes, you do need fixing. Anyone who puts their hands on my niece needs a reckoning." He held Foss's stare in a game of chicken to see who would concede and look away first. Foss was stubborn, but I knew my uncle.

Jens's head whipped around to me. "What's he talking about?"

I shook my head, not wanting to get into it just then. "It's not important." I really couldn't take another fight. Jens was already not speaking to Jamie and was constantly at odds with Charles. I didn't want to deal with yet more drama.

Nik spoke up. "Foss lost his temper and shoved her to the wall with his hands around her throat." He postured and ran his fingers through his sparkly hair. "If I hadn't been there to save her, I shudder to think what the curse would've let him do. I rescued her from his clutches just before she closed her eyes that final time."

Oh, brother.

Mace and Jamie whipped their heads around to gape at me with looks of indignant fury on my behalf. It was sweet, but I shrugged it off as if Foss choking me was no big thing. "I didn't want to whine like a female. Tor hates unnecessary whining," I groused, looking pointedly at the dwarf, who shrank marginally at my chastising.

Fire lit in Jens's green eyes as he moved to stand between Foss and Uncle Rick to gain the angry man's attention. "You and I go way back, so I've been cutting you some slack. She's my charge. You won't compromise my job like that again."

Oh, Jens. Always the romantic.

"She's fine," Foss spat, angry at me, even though I hadn't outed him.

"You'll let Mace take a crack at you," Jens ordered, pointing his finger at his friend. "You'll do it for me. I bailed you out when Olaf tried to buy up the neighboring land around your property to edge you out."

"I paid you back with interest!" Foss countered.

Jens postured. "I helped you out when you couldn't find the thief who was stealing from your vineyards! You owe me, and this is what I want." He pointed his finger to the ground. "And I shouldn't have to bargain with you. All you had to do was ask me for help, and I was there. You should be better than this to me."

Foss looked away, hating having his debts brought up. "Fine. But let it be known I was against this from the beginning. Huldra magic's illegal in Undra."

Uncle Rick chuckled. "I've never known you to be a rule-follower. It's one of the reasons I chose you for this mission. You'll do what has to be done to accomplish your task." He lowered his voice and added the hint of a threat. "I know how you became the fourth power. There's no need to pretend the rules matter to you, though I appreciate the charade for Lucy's sake."

Foss's ears turned red. "Just get on with it," he grumbled. He took a seat on the stone path, crossed his legs and placed his hands on his knees. He would have looked like he was meditating, were it not for the permascowl etched into his face.

Uncle Rick quietly instructed Mace, who looked like he would rather practice on anyone else. Jens, Jamie, Nik, Henry Mancini and Tor all backed into the cave we had set up camp in front of. I wondered when it was that Britta would return with food.

Mace stood, shoulders squared to Foss, who now had his face buried in his hands to fend off having to change his callous ways.

"Cover your ears, everyone. It should only work on Foss, but I'm still learning," Charles instructed. His fingers danced at his sides as if stretching them for a piano recital. His shoulders were tense, and his brow furrowed as he decided how best to start the undoing of Foss.

I covered my ears and watched as Mace whistled for several long seconds, which stretched on into half a minute.

At first, nothing happened. Then Foss began jerking one shoulder, brushing it as if a fly was bothering him. The imaginary fly grew bigger, landing on both shoulders and crawling up his back. He twitched and squirmed on the ground until a sudden burst of air thrust out from his stomach up his body and blasted out of his mouth, as if the curse was a rotting stench in his guts.

I would have thought that was the end of the show, but Mace continued on, mutating his whistle without pausing for breath.

Foss began choking on the air that ran from his body like an exorcism. He pitched forward on all fours and heaved like an animal, looking like a guy bitten by a were-wolf going through his first full-moon transformation. A few more seconds made vomit spew out of him. He growled and spat, seething and twitching until Uncle Rick placed his hand on Mace's wiry shoulder. "That'll do, son."

Charles did not obey, but amped up the whistle, almost in punishment of the man. I watched in horror as Foss clawed at the rock beneath him. His stomach wrenched so violently, I cried out for Mace to stop. I ran in front of him with my hands over my ears and shook my head. "No more! Stop, Charles! Stop it!"

Charles released his hold on the whistle as it died on his lips. He stumbled backwards into Uncle Rick and rubbed his forehead to ease whatever tension that kind of magic inflicted on its user. I knelt down next to Foss and patted his back. "It's okay! It's alright. Deep breaths."

Chemo was a necessary evil that turned many a night into a slumber party on the floor of the bathroom for Linus and me. I brought in a deck of cards, a checkerboard, magazines, dramatic books we liked to replace every third verb with the word "puke", and various other games so Linus didn't have to be alone while he emptied his stomach beyond what one would think might be humanly possible.

Once he went back to school a day too soon and lost his breakfast in the men's room at whatever high school we were going to. I'm thinking it was the one with a wombat mascot. In the middle of first period, I felt something shift in me in that freaky twin way and started to panic. I got a pass and ran to the men's room on a hunch, and found my brother on his hands and knees. There aren't many places more disgusting than a teen boys' public restroom, but I sat on the floor and held my brother until he finished. Then I held him until he finished crying.

Toward the end, our ever-present ability to make even the grimmest circumstance into a joke ran out. Linus was making peace with his impending death, and locked me out one of the times he was throwing up so he could cry by himself. I sat on the other side of the door, listening to his grief, and finally facing a bit of my own. Though he would die, I would live. Life without Linus? I still haven't been able to find anything worse than that.

Though Foss was not Linus and I had no reason to be kind to him, the sight of him vomiting in that awful chemo way tugged me to the ground beside him. My arm went around his back and I pressed his cheek to mine once Foss blasted out his last chunk. "It's okay, Linus. Deep breaths. Take a minute. I've got you."

I could feel Foss's resistance, but in the end, his weakness won out. He sagged against me, his breath coming out in shallow gasps. I ran my fingers through his short black hair, and he closed his eyes, relaxing for just a moment before the world demanded more of him.

Charles cupped his hands together and spilled water out from the center down onto Foss's face. His expression was unmoved at Foss's weakened state as he gulped at the water to rinse his mouth out. After Charles washed away the puke from the rocky path, he knelt down in front of Foss with a serious glare and whispered, "If you put your hands on my sister again, I'll do that all over again just for fun."

Foss sneered as he fought to control his breathing and wriggled out of my hug. "Get off me, Lucy."

Despite the emotion that was raw within me, I smiled and backed away.

Jens helped me to my feet and shook his head. "I guess it didn't work."

I slipped my hand in his. "Sure it did. Uncle Rick said it had to be peeled back in layers. He called me by my name for the first time. I think that's progress."

Foss was resting against the mountain while Uncle Rick checked his eyes and ears, teaching Mace what he did well and what could be improved for the next time.

"Hey, I need a break. I'm going to go see if I can help your sister," I said to Jens, dropping his hand.

"I'll come with you."

I shook my head, tapping my temple. "I have to take Jamie, so why don't you hang out here for a bit."

A hard look took over Jens's features, but he consented. "Don't go far. And take Henry Mancini."

Jamie was already on his feet, wanting to get as far away from the Huldra as he could. Henry Mancini circled us and led the way with his nose to the ground. We walked a little ways up the path, getting just enough distance that we wouldn't be overheard. Jamie shook out his nerves and straightened his shoulders as he spoke. "I know you don't know much about the Huldra, but that was some impressive magic. That he can wield the whistle at all is an anomaly, but to use it to undo a siren's curse? Even stripping off a single layer is incredible. Alrik's right; Mace is a prodigy."

I felt a little proud I was related to someone who was so talented. "Here's hoping it sticks."

Jamie tapped his chest as we walked. "When you get worked up about a matter, I can hear your thoughts quite clearly. I saw your memories. Your brother... Jens loved him, but I can see... I can see."

I nodded, not sure what to say to that. "You must be better at hiding your thoughts, then."

"I'm just more familiar with laplanding. You'll get used to it. I've found putting up a small door in my mind often does the trick. I haven't noticed you wincing when I'm thinking about..." He tried to fish around for a G-rated ending to that sentence. "When I'm thinking about certain people in ungentlemanly ways I shouldn't."

I grimaced. "Oh. Well, I didn't get any of that," I lied. "So kudos on the fake door thing. I'll work on that on my end so you don't have to hear my crap. I don't want you falling in love with Jens, too. Apparently I've got enough competition."

His hand found its way to my back. "It's a privilege to know you, not a burden. You can trust me with your life. I can care for its secrets like they were my own." We walked for a few paces in silence. "Can I trust you with mine?"

"Of course. If you want to talk about your whole Britta/Freya triangle, you can unload on me. I'm good at keeping things to myself." I recalled the mental image I'd fished out of his brain. "And you're right, Freya does have horse's teeth. That, plus the fact that you don't love her? I'd bail." I shook my head like the sage I was. "Ripcord that nonsense, Jamie. Seriously."

Jamie's expression was split between amusement and chagrin. "Thank you. And I can see you've been polite in telling me you can't hear my thoughts. I apologize for anything unseemly you've heard in my head. I'll try to be more discreet."

I stopped and turned to face the world away from the mountain. The light breeze kissed my face as I watched the trees a few stories beneath us sway in their slow-motion grace under the red moon's light. Henry Mancini paused to walk three times around me before licking my shoes. "Well, I guess I'll preemptively apologize in case Jens gets particularly double-jointed in my dreams."

Jamie let out a loud guffaw, his face red at my words. "Yes, well Jens has always been a bit more from your world than mine."

"We'll figure it out," I assured myself more than him.

Britta's steps interrupted our companionable chat, and Jamie stood straighter to greet her.

I tried not to freak out when I saw her with blood dripping from her knife, but I couldn't help it. "Britta! Are you okay? What happened?"

She examined the two kanins in her other hand to see what problem I was talking about. "What? They're properly dead. I'll skin them in a moment. We've already lost the sun, and I didn't want anyone to worry."

"Oh," I said lamely, not knowing how to pass off my horror for pride. "Great job. I'll go let the others know you're safe." I scampered off before Jamie could tag along. *Take your time*, I told him.

I see what you're doing, he replied with a bit of levity in his inner voice. *And thank you.*

12

SHARING DREAMS WITH JAMIE

hen the lovebirds returned to the cave, everything had calmed down marginally. Foss refused to talk to anyone. He hovered in the back of the cave away from any sort of eye contact. Uncle Rick cooked up the kanins for us, and I could hear my mother's gentle nudging about all living things having hearts and feelings as I chewed my gamey bunny. I wasn't a vegetarian, but my mom's heightened conscience poked at my insides. My stomach churned, knowing it needed the protein, but my heart felt sick. There was something about meeting the bunny before you ate it that made it all feel a little uncool.

Jamie kept giving me strange looks, and I knew he was picking up on my swerving conscience. Jens was sullen. His fight with Jamie had gone stale, but neither of them were willing to make the first move. It made for a quiet dining experience.

"I can take first watch," Nik said, raising his hand. "I'm so used to these mountains. Why, once when I was out looking for adventure, I stumbled across a coven of Were-bears. Seven of them, easy. That was a bloody night."

I doubt he's ever fought a Were, Jamie said to my brain. He was practicing sending specific thoughts in hopes of limiting the errant ones. It was a decent plan. *I find his stories taxing.*

Eh, I mentally shrugged. *I kinda think it's cute. His lies don't bother me. They're fun stories. Nik the Man of Valor. It's like having a storyteller traveling with us to tell us entertaining fairytales.*

Nik the Blowhard, Jamie groused. *Weres are hard to kill. When he lies about killing them, it makes Jens's efforts seem easy. Not to mentions ours, too.*

Yes, but Nik does the killing so well. His hair is never out of place. I've seen Jens kill a Were. Messy hair to the extreme. Not as cool.

Jamie chuckled aloud at my joke, but then covered it over with a small cough.

Jens pulled out our sleeping mats while I finished picking at my dinner. I ate enough for my stomach to stop screaming at me in hunger, but handed the rest to Jens when he rejoined us. He'd polished his off quick, and I knew he was still hungry. "You want the rest of my bunny?"

He frowned. "Don't call it that. Kanins aren't rabbits.

Makes me feel like I'm eating Thumper." He eyed the small bones and sighed. "But yes, I'll take whatever part of the bunny you don't want." He sucked down the remnants of my meal and gave the bones to Henry Mancini, who added them to his pile and gnawed happily.

"Goodnight, children," Uncle Rick called to all of us.

Nik grinned, turning from his perch at the mouth of the cave. "Goodnight, father elf."

I smiled at Uncle Rick's happiness at the nickname. His dark skin made the dance of his love all the more evident against the glow of the red moon. He never sired any children, but I knew he'd always wanted a whole litter of sticky hands and crazy schemers.

Jens waved me back toward where Foss was pretending to sleep to stave off his shame at being taken down by a mere whistle. Jens handed me a sleeping mat and motioned to the spot next to him. "I'm beat, Mox. You feel like turning in?"

I nodded, and began moving errant rocks out of the cave to make for a more comfortable sleeping experience. Tor was already snoring on Foss's other side, so I tried to move quietly.

Jamie had gone the gentleman route and cleared away the stones for Britta. When I noticed the difference between Jamie's level of consideration for Britta, and Jens's lack of awareness, I gave an internal sigh, wondering if I'd be in a relationship long enough one day where the man would clear the rocks away for me.

When I came back from my second load of rock removal, I saw Jamie clearing the rest of my spot for me. I stopped short, my heart moved at his small act of kindness. *You didn't have to do that, Jamie. That was real sweet of you. Thank you.*

He tipped his head to me. *Jens will learn,* he assured me. *Give him time.*

I tried to brush off the comment. *Oh, it's fine. I don't need all that gentleman stuff. It's good you're doing that for Britt, though. I can tell she appreciates it.*

He spoke to me as an older brother might, teaching me the ways of the world with his sage wisdom. *Being a gentleman isn't as much for Britta's benefit as it is for mine. The harder I try to deserve her, the more I someday might.*

I had never heard such sweet, altruistic words, and I was glad someone as great as Jamie wasn't wasted on a girl who didn't appreciate him. The two laid down next to each other with matching scandalous grins on their faces at the social rules they were breaking by sleeping on separate mats next to each other. Totally precious.

I laid down on my sleeping mat in between Britta and Jens, pecking Jens on the cheek before beginning the long process of clearing out Jamie's thoughts from my head, as well as my own.

I dreamt of Jens. Though he wasn't double-jointed in this dream, he was romantic. He took me out to a nice restaurant, the kind where you feel like an inexperienced kid no matter how old you get. He pulled out my chair, held open doors, and made polite conversation that had nothing to do with Weres.

It made sense that I dreamed of normal. My everyday was anything but.

Midway through the soup course, my dream was hijacked, like someone else had gotten ahold of the remote.

Jamie was making out with Britta on his bed, gold curtains swinging out to christen their passionate union. Britta made soft noises of love, and Jamie let out manly grunts laced with lust.

I tried not to look, but I couldn't figure out how to get out of his dream and back to my date, so I sat in the corner and faced the red wall, hoping we'd snap out of this quick.

Then I heard screaming in the room. "No! No!"

I whirled around and found Jamie in horror at whatever he'd just done. "Britta, no!"

He was still holding her body in a passionate embrace, as he had been doing during their make-out session, but instead of kissing him, Britta's mouth began to disintegrate. Blood poured out from her teeth, and like acid, the bloody drool melted off bits of her face, caving her head in as she wilted away in Jamie's arms like a crumbling flower.

"I'm sorry! I'm sorry! Britta, no!" He fought to put her back together, but the more he touched her, the more she fell apart like a sandcastle.

With tears in his eyes, he looked around and saw me for the first time. "I killed her! My kiss killed her!"

I ran to him, prying his hands off her clothes that were melting and crumbling through his fingers. "No, Jamie. Oh, honey. No, no. It's just a dream. A really terrible dream." I wrapped my arms around him and squeezed. "It's alright. We'll wake up soon."

He shook violently in my arms. "This is when it happens! It's happening! Right after I kill someone in my dreams from loving them too much, I try to do it in real life. Lucy, you have to help me! I can't stop my body!"

I began to understand the depth of Jamie's curse. I took Jamie away from the bed and pushed open the door, revealing my boring date Jens had not noticed I was missing from. "Come over to my dream. Britta's fine. You would never hurt her in real life. Your brain's just messing with you."

Since we were dreaming and could not be held accountable for our actions, Jamie sat at the table with Jens and me and wept, the strong man turning into a scared boy.

Dream Jens didn't notice the turn of events. He merely asked if I wanted more wine.

I loved dream Jens.

The two of us ate, indulging in pleasant conversation until Jamie felt well enough to join us. Jamie ate a roll and looked around my dream, asking questions about what every little device and oddity was.

It was boring, but Jamie started to relax at the soothing uneventful dream he had the option of escaping to. He laid his head down on the table, letting me relax him by running my fingers through his chestnut curls.

The night faded into morning, and I awoke to Britta sitting up, watching Jamie sleep. Her expression was wistful, but also filled with concern.

"Hey," I whispered. "Did he attack you last night?"

She turned, offering up a half smile. "Good morning, sister. No, he had a bad dream, though. He got worked up, and that's usually when he strikes. He starts panting in his sleep, and then gets up and attacks." She turned her attention back onto Jamie. "Jens tells me dreaming is normal where you come from, but here it's a curse."

"It's so strange to me that Undrans don't dream. Nothing at all happens in your mind when you go to sleep?"

Britta shook her head. "His father's afraid of him because of it. If word got out about his affliction, everyone would be afraid, too."

"Huh."

She bit back a grin. "Foss's afraid of you for it, too."

My eyes widened as I stretched. "Wow. Superpower I didn't even know about. Dreaming's no big thing in my world. Everyone does it almost every night."

Tor shuddered and whispered over his shoulder from the mouth of the cave where he'd taken Nik's post halfway through the night. "It's not normal, scheming up plans while ya sleep. Yer dangerous, female."

I chuckled and sat up, frowning at the empty space beside me. "Where's Jens?"

"Making sure we weren't followed and trying to hunt us up more food. He's used to your food now, and hasn't lived off the trail in a long time."

Jamie stirred, his eyes fluttering open and landing on Britta's adoring face. Emotion so heady welled up in him and clenched my gut, too. He reached his hand up and cupped her cheek, pulling her down for a simple kiss.

"Jamie!" she admonished him, her head darting around to see if anyone was looking.

I kept my eyes on my lap. Tor kept focused on the stillness of nature outside the cave so they could have their moment while everyone else slept.

Jamie's voice was thick with all the things he wanted to say to her, but couldn't in proper company. "Cursed though I am, I'm blessed every time I see your face."

It was a simple compliment, but given the nightmare he'd just endured, I swooned on her behalf.

"I didn't hurt anyone in the night?"

Britta shook her head. "At one point you looked like you might, but you calmed down. You're learning to control it," she said, hero-worship clear in her voice.

Jamie turned and looked over at me, wondering if my part in his nighttime musings was imagined, or if we had the same account of the night. I gave him a thumbs up and nodded, letting him know that we'd gotten through the upset together just fine.

His chest heaved with relief and joy. *Do you know what this means?* he asked, trepidation making him almost too nervous to believe this happiness was attainable. *We found a way around my curse! If I can come over into your dreams, I can escape mine.* He closed his eyes in reverent respect for our connection. *Thank you, Lucy. You saved me.*

I nodded again, keeping my eyes on my lap so our conversation would remain between us. *You can thank me by making out with Britta for real someday. I told you we'd find a way through this.* I cast up a half-smile. *I'll share my dreams with you any day.*

13

THE TRUTH ABOUT NIK

It had been six days of traversing around the fat mountain. Six days of Britta sleeping holding onto Jamie's hand, lest he hulk out in his sleep and attack us. Six nights of Jamie crossing over into my subconscious, and me altering my dream to accommodate him. Six days of crusty bread, berries and water, that is until Jens caught and skinned four more kanins. Jamie and Jens were still not speaking, nor would they look at each other.

Charles and Jens were being pissy with each other, too. They'd fought over Huldra magic and when it should be used. They bickered about how my arm should be wrapped, and were still sore about it when I stomped off and took care of it myself.

We were on our way to Nøkken, which meant that Nik was all about educating us on his greatness, as if we hadn't heard every amazing story about him a zillion times already. That didn't make for extra smiles as we traveled, though I still thought his stories were sweet.

We migrated down the mountain on the far side from the Warf, coming closer to ground level, even though it took a little longer. There was rumored to be several nests of those creepy spiders up there, so Uncle Rick voted we not take our chances this time. We were nearing the path to Nøkken as we exited the mountain, and there was a mixture of emotions about that. The air was ripe with tension, relief and a touch of fear.

I was so glad I had my regular clothes, including my sneakers. The dresses came with sandals that were not built for day-long hikes. Not that my Chucks had a crap ton of padding, but still.

Charles moved to my other side (Jens was permanently affixed to my right) with a hesitant expression. His voice was quiet, as if he was afraid his question might evoke a storm. "Am I allowed to ask you about our mother? It's just that I don't have many memories of her, and I always wanted a bigger picture."

"Of course." I swallowed down my immediate flood of flight that came over me whenever I was forced to talk about my family. My arms banded around my stomach as we walked and talked. "She's taller than me. About your height. Hair like yours. She was funny. Smiled a lot."

"What else?"

"I dunno. What else can you say about a person? She was great. Giant hippie. Awesome cook. Vegetarian, but could whip up a mean pot roast for the rest of us. Always knew when Linus and I were up to no good. She had this game when we were acting up. Linus and I had to go to separate rooms and try to think of a number between one and twenty, write it down and try to sync our brains until we came up with the same one."

"Did it work?" he asked, his curiosity evident. "I've not met any twins my age before. It's not common on our side. They only come from Huldra women, so after they were banished, no more were born here, only on your side. It's a fifty percent chance a Huldra'll give birth to twins."

"Oh, really? Huh."

I mentally cataloged all the twins that had popped up, knowing statistically the number had increased by a wide margin in the past two decades. If every set of twins was the result of a Huldra procreating in my world, I couldn't imagine how many there were that got kicked out of Undraland so long ago.

I tried to get back to the conversation at hand. "Linus and I had about a seventy percent success rate, but our brains have always been on the same wavelength." I pressed my arms to my stomach and held myself tighter.

"It must've been difficult to lose him."

I laughed with no humor in the sound. "No. Difficult is this mountain. Difficult was figuring out how to pick myself up and live on my own. Life without Linus is... Everything was impossible for a long time. It's hard to make people understand without them thinking I'm being dramatic."

"Try me," Charles challenged as he climbed over a particularly large obstruction along our path.

"It's like suddenly going through a quadruple amputation and a head injury. All the things only your best friend knows are useless, because he's gone. It's like you can't complete a thought, because he always knew the other half of it. And then everyone expects you to do all the things you could do before you had the quadruple amputation, so you learn to." I shook my head. "I'm not explaining it right."

"I'm keeping up. Do you need help getting across?" he inquired, offering his hand. It would have been easier to get past the uneven rocky surface if I could use my hands for climbing, but they were frozen around my stomach, and I did not think I could move them without my personal guts spilling out all over the place.

Jens understood. His arm went around my back to steady me as we made it across to level rock. The hollow feeling in my bones set in, and I fished for a change of topic. "How about you? What was it like with Uncle Rick?"

Charles put on a polite smile. "It was nice."

Uncle Rick spoke over his shoulder to us. "Charles is being kind. It's miserable for him. I was not home as often as I should've been when he was young. I was a wretched parental replacement, focusing more on developing his magic than taking him out to play."

"You were fine," Charles allowed graciously. "And it's not like you could've taken me to play with other children."

"Why not?" I demanded.

Mace's face twisted to a malodorous grimace. "I'm a half-breed. Not many parents wanted me around their kids. And the few that were willing to give it a try at first changed their minds when I was not a joy to be around, what with being abandoned and all."

I knew I could not, but I wanted to hold him, scratch his back to soothe him for hours as he confessed his childhood to me. He was so lonely, even now. I could tell he wanted more information, but was being sensitive to the fact that I was wussing out.

I clutched my stomach and muscled onward. "If it helps, we didn't stay in one place long enough to make many friends. We picked up and moved at least twice a year. Sometimes it wasn't even worth unpacking. But I had Linus, so it's not the same. I'm sorry you were so alone. That's not cool."

He offered me a small curve of his lips. "But now I have you, so life is sunshine again."

I noticed Foss shooting Jens a wary look. Jens stomped ahead to converse quietly with him.

Uncle Rick fell back to walk with Charles and me. "I'm glad to see you two getting along. Charles, perhaps you could educate Lucy about trolls. They don't exist where she comes from."

"Really? Wow." He scratched his head. "Trolls are around twenty feet tall, strong as an ox and mean as a bull. They travel in herds usually. They eat things our size, including us. Skin us like kanin and eat us raw. They don't bother the civilized nations much, and usually feed on wild animals out between countries." He turned to Uncle Rick. "Oh, great. Is that what's coming next?"

Uncle Rick nodded. "Nik caught a whiff of them coming from up ahead."

"How many?" Mace asked, cracking his fingers as if readying his magic.

"At least twelve." Uncle Rick placed his hand on Mace's shoulder. "Let Jens and Foss handle it. Hopefully you will not need to get involved."

"I can help," Charles countered, eager to display his power. "I've been studying for years, and I know which whistles to use."

Uncle Rick touched his ears. "You forget the one detail that makes Jens and Foss a better fit for this job. Trolls are hard of hearing. A Huldra whistle won't do much to them if they can't hear it." He mussed Mace's black hair. "I prefer you stay with Lucy."

Charles deflated and walked closer to me, hands shoved in his pockets.

"You alright?" I asked, keeping my voice quiet.

Mace spoke with an edge to him. "I guess. I get to look useless while Jens is the hero."

I bumped my shoulder to him. "Better than being actually useless, like me. I think it's cool that you're the secret weapon. Stay close."

Charles chuckled. "I'm sure it's nothing as glamorous as you make it sound. But I can't think of a better place to be than by your side." He gave me a look that was so sincere, it made me want to turn away in case he could see right through me. "And you're not useless."

"Aw. You're a sweet little liar."

Nik stopped walking up ahead and turned to address the group with his hands raised to garner our attention. His gaze was averted, and I could tell he was nervous. "Okay. Here's the thing. There's a group of trolls up ahead." For once, he did not look like he was the most perfect man ever to grace our presence. His haughty expression gave way to regret and insecurity, and I noticed sweat beading at his bluish white brow as his feet shuffled from side to side. "The thing is, you don't know these trolls like I do."

Mace's eyebrows knit together as he tried to decipher Nik's meaning. "What's there to know? A troll's a troll."

For the first time, Nik was uncomfortable. He massaged the nape of his neck as he tried to find the right words. "Being the celebrity I am, I sometimes come to these mountains for some peace and quiet."

I could feel Jens mentally rolling his eyes in perfect synchronicity with Foss's actually rolled eyes.

"Those rumors about trolls are somewhat true, but not of the ones in the tribe you're about to meet. If you treat them like normal people, they'll be friendly to you.

If you treat them like monsters, they'll... Well, the rumors you heard will become true. So no shouting. No looking at them like they're scary or hideous. They're quite sensitive. And civilized. In fact," he said, wringing his hands. "Jamie and Lucy, if you could play up your royalty, that would help a lot. And I'm not sure how they'll take to Henry Mancini. It would really help if we brought them a gift."

Foss nodded. "Would a few kanin help?" He stopped and frowned at Nik. "Wait. You're famous for ridding your land of trolls. How do your special friends feel about that?"

And here it came. I could almost guess the words that tumbled out of his mouth before they reached me. "I did get rid of them. Some of the stories of my methods may have been... exaggerated."

"By you!" Foss yelled, pointing his finger in accusation. "This is why my people hate the Nøkken. All talk, no substance. All this time you've filled our heads with nothing but lies. How much of it all is true?"

Nik held his head up high. "I did rid our land of trolls. The tribe I came across agreed to move so they would not be a bother to us. They keep an eye on the territory to make certain other, more traditional trolls don't infiltrate our land. In exchange, I bring tea and sit for afternoons with them, educating them about society life. The trolls stay where they are, and the Nøkken land is spared their occasional rage."

Tor was red with fury. Jens shrugged at me and shook

his head, as if he'd expected as much. When Jamie tried to cast him a similar look, Jens scowled at him.

Yes. I'm traveling with a bunch of children. I clapped my hands together three times to reel in the building arguments. "It doesn't matter. I don't want to be caught on this mountain overnight anymore, so let's all chill and focus. Foss, why don't you and Jens hunt up a bunny or Bambi or something they'll think is delicious. Get some space. Nik, tell Uncle Rick, Tor and Mace what you know about these trolls, in case anything goes south and you need help. Britt, could you and Jamie pick some of those wild berries? I'm medium starving, so I know you're all ravenous." I motioned to a bush a little ways off. "They're not poisonous, are they? I don't really know about that kinda thing."

Britta nodded gratefully and tugged Jamie off away from Jens. "Right away, Lucy. Great idea." She pointed her finger toward the mountain and waved her brother off toward it.

Foss grumbled. "I'll not be ordered around by a rat."

"Hop to it, princess. Make yourself useful." I snapped my fingers just to irritate Foss, knowing he wouldn't beat on me in front of Jens.

Foss's expression mutated, looking like he'd just sucked on a lemon. "Get ahold of your woman, Jens!"

Jens started off in the direction he deemed best for hunting. "If only that was possible. You heard her, princess. Time to go a'hunting."

When Foss and Jens started picking on Nik, I donned

my mother's get-to-bed voice and barked, "Ripcord outta here, or you don't want to know what!"

Jens turned to me with a cocky expression, arms crossed over his chest. "You know, I think I do. What exactly are you going to do if we give Nik grief for being a pompous tool? I mean, killing a troll is no joke. It's a lot of work and it's deadly. He walks around like it's nothing. Like what we actually did is the same as what he did in his head."

I scowled at Jens. "Martin Luther King would be proud of Nik using words and diplomacy to solve his problems rather than warmongering."

"Warmongering?!" Jens shouted in astonishment, our playful jeers mutating into an actual fight. "I fought because there was no other option. My parents and a slew of other people left for Be on account of those trolls! And how much exactly did your precious leader's words mean when you and Jamie killed that bear and ruined your lives? Good luck getting your white picket fence now!"

As soon as the words left him, I could see the regret on his face. I shirked back from him as if his words had grown a hand and slapped me.

"That's too far, Jens!" Mace growled.

Uncle Rick clapped his hands twice, giving the argument a sense of finality. "Lucy, what a wonderful idea for Jens and Foss to acquire a gift for our gracious hosts. Be on your way, gentlemen. We'll wait for you here."

"Loos, I'm sorry. I didn't mean that."

"On your way, Jens," Uncle Rick repeated. "Perhaps if you look hard enough, you'll find some common sense in the bushes over yonder." He motioned to a thicket that was quivering at the base.

Foss was already on his way with Henry Mancini.

I let out a shriek of surprise when Jens snatched up a bunny and broke its neck without a flinch. "This, Nik! This is what you told us all you did to the trolls. Use reason to get them to stop invading. Fine. But don't lie about it. Don't carry on like you're some big war hero. What qualifies you to even be on this trip, other than that we needed a random Nøkken for the portal?"

I sat down on a bed of moss and leaned against the mountain, wishing for a mattress and a pillow. Though it was only early evening, I was weary from everything and everyone. The gullin, the sleeping on rock, sharing my subconscious with Jamie, the fighting. Mostly the fighting.

I hugged my knees to my chest and picked at the bandage on my arm. My head started to ache a little, but I ignored it, figuring Jamie would feel the tether and trail back a few feet.

When I was sick, my dad would cook his famous chicken soup with handmade noodles. Mom would whip up a purple cold remedy concoction in the blender that fizzed and somehow tasted creamy. I'd never known what she put in it. Now that she was gone, I prayed I would never get a cold. Linus would keep me entertained by making up disgusting mad libs, using "butt" as often as possible. When he inevitably caught my cold, I was in charge of the mad libs. My noun of choice was usually pus, which could also be verbed in a pinch if you played it fast and loose with the English language just to get a laugh out of your brother.

When we were too weak to protest more than an irritated groan, Dad would read Shakespeare to us, with Mom acting out some of the parts so we understood what was going on. Linus liked to add in inappropriate sound effects. I liked to pretend I understood what the story was about. Linus and I would redirect the endings of the tragedies to be comedies, and the love stories to have dramatic soap opera twists of a surprise half-brother or something of that sort. I looked up at Charles and couldn't help but think how funny Linus would find the dramatic twists in my new life.

But he wasn't here. He was lost without me, just as I felt lost without him. I stroked the small heart-shaped container of ashes on my necklace, letting the motion soothe me. Part of me was secretly hoping I might reunite with my mother on the other side, since Pesta apparently took her into Be after using my dad's bones to construct her portal. Uncle Rick said it would be impossible to see her without losing my soul and forfeiting my right arm, but the lure was there. As horrific as it sounded, there was very little life for me here.

14

BJORN

Nik was the only one with a smile when the nineteen-foot-tall giant dressed in tattered shorts and a brown knitted shawl came out of his cave to greet us. I was the shrimp amongst all the tall people as it was. To stand next to someone more than three times my height and several times my thickness made my heart pound.

There was a conversation between Nik and the giant hunchbacked, but muscular, man. Then there was small talk involving pleasantries about the weather and town gossip. I'm sure his name was mentioned, but I was too entranced by his appearance. He looked sort of normal, but with slight alterations. His skin was tinged greenish, like he was sick or something. His back was shaped like an old man's, but he appeared limber in his movements, and strong enough to lift an elephant. I expected him to speak like Andre the Giant, but he sounded sort of Swedish. His feet were bare and clubbed, with the green almost as dark as grass around his toes like a fungus. His hands were as long as my torso with fingers like crazy long bananas that were still green at the stems.

The three kanins Foss and Jens had brought him as a gift now seemed like barely an appetizer. I picked up Henry Mancini and clutched him to my chest.

Nik introduced me, but my mouth went dry. "H-Hello, sir."

"Are humans just skinny dwarves then?" Bjorn looked at me quizzically. "Prettier. Less filthy?"

Nik answered for me, since apparently I'd grown unbearably shy. "Queen Lucy is the finest of her race, Bjorn. She's been hand-picked by me for a top-secret mission."

This earned me an appreciative nod. He moved surprisingly quickly for someone so large and oddly shaped.

Nik lowered his voice in a gentle scold, "And remember our little talk on making personal remarks? Very uncivilized."

Bjorn stood straighter, chagrinned. "A thousand apologies, Queen Lucy." He bowed and almost knocked Tor over with the movement.

I waved off his apology with a shaky hand. "No problem. This is a lovely place you have here. I mean, these are the best trees I've seen in a while." It was meant as polite conversation, but it was also true. The trees on the other side of the path from the mountain were tall with thick trunks and knotted roots that looked like something out of a Tim Burton movie. The roots wound around each other, almost holding hands in nature's snuggle.

Nik placed his hand atop Bjorn's, since that was the only place he could be reached. "Would you mind terribly if we passed through your territory along the path, old friend? We're in a bit of a hurry."

Bjorn looked over his shoulder, and I could see a few of the trunks shifting slightly. Upon closer inspection, I saw some of the bark was not part of a tree at all, but it was worn as armor by a group of trolls who were too afraid to come greet us. It was kinda cute. "We'll let you pass." Bjorn held out a large hand to Uncle Rick, who looked amazingly small next to the man. "Alrik. I've heard of your adventures from Nik. Good to meet you."

"I'm sure the pleasure is mine. I'm afraid Nik's been keeping us quite busy on his errand. He's very wise. A pleasure to be chosen for his journey, and a pleasure to be led to your land. Two pleasures in one visit. I'm a fortunate elf, indeed." Uncle Rick's gracious diplomacy was a beautiful thing to watch in action.

Bjorn grinned, revealing his good nature and about five missing teeth. "Does your secret mission have to do with those elk I showed you, Nik?" Then he turned to Uncle Rick. "Nik didn't believe me at first."

"Yes, well, Nik's logic knows no bounds. Yes. We're

examining all sorts of animals with souls implanted in them." Uncle Rick turned to us. "Nik told me of an alleged Were-elk Bjorn discovered in these very mountains." He gave Bjorn and Nik a sweeping bow.

Nik slapped Bjorn on the lower back in camaraderie. "Thank you for letting us pass by your river and saving us a trip up in the mountains. We plan on taking your news of the Were-elk to the Nøkken, now that we have enough proof. "

Bjorn nodded. "Nik, do you think it wise to take the women with you by the river?" He looked at Britta and me warily. "That seems like playing with fire."

Nik nodded. "We're in a bit of a hurry. We'll be careful with them."

Bjorn wrung his hands together and lowered his voice. "We've been getting trouble from our neighbors to the north." He pointed up the mountain to an opening several stories above. "Nik, I was hoping maybe you could reason with them."

Nik swallowed. "I can certainly do that. Could it wait until next week? We're a bit pressed for time. Top-secret mission and all."

Bjorn's hand went over his heart, looking like an old lady. "Oh, goodness. Of course. It can wait. Just a little territory dispute. They don't like us using the path, but I'm sure they won't mind that you use it. Just please be careful when you're passing by the river. There've been more of the Nøkkendalig since the jailbreak last week."

"Jailbreak?" Nik asked, clearly not in the know. "Who escaped?"

"Most of the Nøkkendalig. That's what I was trying to tell you. None of your people have come to wrangle them back up. They're just turning their heads and ignoring the problem. I'd watch this one and the other very closely, if I were you."

I was very aware of Britta's gasp and her fist clenching the garment over her breasts.

"What are the Nøkkendalig?" I inquired, my voice still mousy. "And what would they want with me and Britt?"

Bjorn looked at me like I had just asked him who the Beatles were.

Nik's voice was grave as he spoke. "Each of the Undraland races received a curse when Pesta was locked away in Be. The group of Nøkken warriors who helped put her away bear her curse, and pass it onto their children. Nøkken are great swimmers, but the Nøkkendalig were forced to live underwater. They've become a gang of anarchists who operate outside the law. Some say they work for Pesta, making life so unbearable that young women flock to Be as soon as they come of age."

Bjorn smiled sadly. "And they want what any evil man wants from a pretty young woman."

Gross.

My palms began to sweat, and I made my way nearer to Jens, disregarding our fight.

His arm banded around my shoulders, keeping me close without conveying any of his fears.

"Why are there always rapists?" I whispered while Nik and Bjorn conversed about the best way to get through to Nøkken. "I mean, seriously. Shouldn't all societies have evolved past that by now?"

Jens kissed my temple. "Why you ever worry about anything when I'm around is beyond me. I've got you."

I wanted to run and hide, but with evil giants above, evil golden boars behind, and the evil Nøkkendalig ahead, there weren't many good places to go. I inched Mace to stand in front of me, and he postured.

Bjorn pointed his enormous finger up the mountain. "Be careful of the Northerners. They probably won't attack you, but best not test it, all the same. They're not civilized."

I gulped.

Pleasantries were exchanged, bunnies were given, and the dangerous water-lined pathway to Nøkken was granted to us. I curtsied to Bjorn as I passed, still very nervous he might accidentally crush me with his giant hands.

15

AN AFTERNOON OF TROLL-SLAYING

It was understood that there would be no talking when we left the cluster of trees Bjorn claimed as his. I wanted to ask a million questions, but the atmosphere was too tense. Nik led the way with Tor along the brook, their swords unsheathed. Foss and Jamie walked on either side of the invisible Britta, while Jens and Charles flanked me, with Uncle Rick taking up the rear. Jens held my hand, turning us both invisible as we plodded forward on silent feet.

Then it occurred to me: they were protecting us from the Nøkkendalig in the water and the mean trolls up in the mountain straight above us. I kept my eyes down on Henry Mancini and trudged forward, trying to think invisible thoughts.

I checked in with Jamie, looking through his eyes to see that Britta was trembling. Every step she took was laced with fear. Charles was sweating. I hugged Henry Mancini tight as I walked down what felt like death row.

Then it happened. A boulder the size of an elevator tumbled down the side of the mountain right for the head of the group. Britta screamed as Jamie yanked her aside while Foss and Nik scattered.

"Now we've done it!" Nik shouted. "Can you get around?" he asked Jens, glancing at the narrow space of grass the elevator-sized boulder did not take up on the path.

"We can, but she can't. Too close to the water," Jens ruled. "Up and over. Foss, you ready?"

Before anyone consulted me, Jens handed Henry Mancini to Charles and then lifted me off the ground. "Climb over," he ordered.

I scrambled to hitch my leg on top of the rock, but another boulder the size of a sedan came pitching through the air right for me. I dropped back down next to Jens, who covered my body with his as the car shattered on the elevator. Rocks pelted him from the collision, but it didn't seem to hurt him; it only pissed him off. His fist pounded into the ground next to my head. "That's it!" Jens stood, machete drawn. "Foss, you with me?"

"I'm already there. How many, Nik?"

Nik was positively ashen. "Seven."

"Jens, no!" Britta screamed.

Jens and Foss jumped up the mountain. I mean, literally jumped. I'd never seen anything so graceful and just, well, dangerous. Tiny crevices were preselected in their brains as they dashed up the mountain to the cave the boulders had launched from.

My hands clawed at my face as I watched, afraid to look, but unable to look away. There was shouting. There was slashing. There was crashing. I was a ball of angst until Charles interrupted my anxiety. "We need to get to the other side of this boulder," he reminded me. "Vanish her, Jamie! She shouldn't be seen!"

"Jamie! Take Henry Mancini," I instructed as Charles placed my poor afraid puppy on top of the elevator-shaped rock.

Jamie snatched him down and handed him off to Nik. "You're next, Lucy."

Mace's hands were on my hips, and he hoisted me up. This time I found my footing quickly, crawled over and jumped down into Jamie's strong arms. Charles and Uncle Rick were thankfully able to climb up themselves and jump down. All we needed were the two warriors in the cave. I glanced behind me to make sure I wasn't too near the water.

"Lucy! Keep your head down. Eyes shut if you have to." Jamie ordered, snatching up my hand so I disappeared.

"What am I not supposed to look at? I have no idea what's going on. Where are the Nøkkendalig?" My voice had that high-pitched squeaky quality it got whenever I was freaking out.

A skeleton the size of Nik launched out of the cave above. It had been picked clean.

Jamie hugged Britta's head to his chest, burying her sobbing face in his shirt to hide her already invisible eyes. He gripped the back of my head and did the same to me.

I reached out to Britta and squeezed her arm. "He'll come back, Britta. Jens is crazy strong. It'll be okay." Though my words were meant to encourage, fear dampened any help they might do.

It was twenty more harrowing minutes I willed my words to be true. I could feel Britta's crazed fear, and it began to transfer to me. Jamie clutched us both tighter, burying our faces so deep in his chest, I was beginning to grow hot.

Finally we heard slow movements descending down the mountain, and Jamie let out a gust of elation. "Are you well?" he called.

Jens answered, "I'd be better if I could get a burger around here. I'm so sick of apples and rolls. Just you wait till we go to the Other Side. Chinese food all the way. I'm buying."

I could tell by his bravado that he was hurt, but trying to hide it. Britta struggled like a butterfly against Jamie and ran to the foot of the mountain to greet her brother. Jamie followed behind.

Foss had been tossed around pretty good and bore the beginnings of several bruises. Jens looked about the same, but he'd also been knocked in the head, which he held through Britta's examination. "We've got to get out of here," he warned, standing up straight. He reached inside his shirt and pulled out the small pouch he kept around his neck. He took a pinch of the lavender powder inside and clamped it to his nose, inhaling it like medicine. "You need some?" he offered to Foss.

"I'm not hurt, and I'm not a junkie," Foss grumbled, nursing his side. "Let's go. That last one was mostly dead, but I didn't stick around to confirm it." He limped forward and led the way down the narrow grassy path that ran between the river and the mountain.

"Head down, Loos," Jens commanded, grabbing my hand to turn me invisible. "But after we get through this, I'll be wanting my hero's kiss for saving your life there."

"Is that so? Well, if we get through all this, remind me of this exact moment. You can hold out till then, right?" I motioned to Britta, who was crying softly on Jamie's shoulder. "Go hug her. She was shaking like a leaf waiting for you to come back. She loves you."

Jens pecked my cheek and trotted ahead to hug his sister and let her fawn over his wounds.

It happened so fast, I didn't have time to brace myself. I was a couple feet away from the water's edge when a man's slimy hand lunged out of the brook and grabbed hold of my ankle. I screamed as I was yanked off my feet and dragged under the water. The last thing I saw was Mace's horrified expression as I slipped through his fingers.

16

NØKKENDALIG

espite the warmth of the sun, the water was ice cold, but that was not the thing I focused on. I was dragged several feet down toward the seemingly bottomless bottom of the river before I got a good look at my attackers. Seven men with white-blue hair like Nik's surrounded me as I struggled fruitlessly against the grip on my ankle. One of them with a hooked nose and pierced ears pinched my nose as he held my thrashing head still. He covered his mouth with mine and filling my lungs with air so I could be awake for the whole degradation.

I writhed and jerked my body around, but they closed in on me, limiting my movements.

I caught a glimpse of Britta a few feet away, surrounded by her own group of cursed Nøkken men. She was screaming and struggling to free herself from them. She stabbed one with her knife, but there were so many more that crowded around her.

Then I heard the singing. Deep, melodious voices boomed underwater, commanding us to stop struggling. Their power didn't work on me, but I saw Britta go from fighting with her knife to floating between them like a lifeless doll.

I screamed into the hook-nosed man's mouth.

The seven tall Nøkken men closed in on me, confused as to why I wasn't going limp and making their depravity easier to indulge in. I felt my shirt lift up past my ribs, my flesh burning like sizzling steak where their slippery hands touched me. I tried to escape, but I knew I didn't stand a chance. Hands grabbed me, groped at me and pulled at my limbs, burning as they touched. I screamed in the murky abyss to no avail. I'd never known fear as I did in that moment.

The man who was singing turned to me and smiled as I struggled to keep my jeans from being parted from me.

Then a white light filled the water throughout the entire brook. The only thing I saw was white, but I didn't need sight to know which way was up. I pushed forward and felt around for Britta, panicking when I made my presence known to her attackers. I reached around and located her hand, but it was no good. I was pulled away from her by the vicious men just as I felt my lungs were about to burst.

The water pressed in around me as the burning hands pulled me further under. I saw nothing, felt nothing, was nothing in that moment. As my shirt was removed from my body, I once again made peace with my life coming to an early end.

17

ESCAPE

*H*ands were on me, pumping my sternum in earnest as water pushed itself out of my lungs and into Mace's hand as if it had been summoned there.

Nik's wet hair was the first thing I saw, and then his worried face as he turned me on my side to cough up the rest of the fluid. People were talking to me, but I didn't have it in me to answer. I simply laid there in my jeans and bra, curled up in the fetal position and watched as the world reintroduced itself to me. Jens was next to Jamie, who was coughing like he'd been the one dunked underwater. Uncle Rick was farther away, running a sopping wet Britta from the brook toward our destination as she wept.

"They're alive! Let's move!" Foss ordered. He hoisted Jamie up, and motioned for Jens to be a crutch for the prince's other arm.

Nik lifted me up off the ground and carried me like a baby as he ran us in their direction. Charles carried Henry Mancini behind us, horror washing over his face.

Everyone was a mess of emotions, but I felt nothing. My face was blank as Nik carried me, running for over a mile. I should have been embarrassed at my partial nakedness. I should have been crying at the hands that I could still feel on me. I should have had some sort of reaction, but all I did was watch Nik's wet white-blue hair flapping and sparkling in the breeze. I could see his fear, but I was immune to it, completely checked out from reality.

Nik ran at full speed until the brook disappeared and we were surrounded by old fashioned German-looking buildings. Little wooden houses with ornate shutters and colored doors whizzed by me. He did not stop until we entered a large orange house and the white door slammed shut behind us.

"Niklas! Gracious, what's all this? Who are your friends? Is she dead? Oh, Niklas! Look at the new drapes I got. Fancy lace from the east village."

"Great, mom. Lucy!" Niklas laid me on the couch and checked my vitals.

"Niklas! The couch, dear. She's all wet. Could you move her to the floor?" The chubby woman had hair like Nik's, but hers was coifed and set to look extra fancy. She turned to Charles and caught sight of his tail and elfish features. "Ah! Niklas! What are you thinking? Get the halfy out of my house! Out, before the neighbors see! Out!" She swatted Mace with her plump hand. Uncle Rick stood in between them, his gentle expression resolute that Charles would not be struck.

Nik ignored his mother. "She's alive. Why isn't she moving?"

Wasn't I? My body felt too heavy to budge, so I stopped trying to access my limbs. I stared blankly at whoever came in my vision. Jens. Foss. Uncle Rick. Charles. Whatever. My brain was fuzzy. I couldn't find myself in the fog, so I let myself float. Jens tore his shirt off and pushed it over my head. It smelled amazing. Like man and cookies and warm comfort. Then I was pushed into the warmth, and my soul felt the growing heat. My body had left me, but at least I could still feel my soul. My wet shoes and jeans were yanked off me, and then I was floating again. Nik with his wet, but still bouncing, game show host hair moved me to a bed that was so soft, I could have sworn it was pure feathers. A comforter was pulled over me and tucked up to my chin. Somebody was holding my hand, but I couldn't focus enough to tell who.

I drifted in my mind to one of the times I was getting picked on in Junior High. Erin Hanson filled my locker with shaving cream, ruining my books and homework. She'd also written "ditz" on my locker in permanent marker that the janitor took two months to paint over. Every day for two months was a reminder that I was stupid, and had no friends.

Erin Hanson had a crush on Linus and thought picking

on me would be a good way to get on his radar. I'll never understand women like that. I'd had a paper on the Civil War due that day, and stayed up late with my dad to finish it.

Linus's retaliation when the school took too long to clean my locker was to write a very offensive slur on Erin's locker, which, I'll admit, did speed things along as far as getting them to bust out the locker paint. He also filled her locker with deck stain, ruining her property far worse than mine. I loved him for it. I loved him for a great many reasons. He was my best friend, and in many cases, my only friend.

I remember being covered in shaving cream up to my elbows and all over the front of my only non-resale purchased shirt, but Linus held me anyway. We sat on the floor in the hall as I cried into his shirt that day, certain it couldn't get any worse than that.

If only I'd known.

My body ached, but I didn't care enough to address the pain. Instead, I screamed in my mind. Over and over, screamed for my brother to find me. Screamed for my dad to take me home. I didn't care which home. Just somewhere with Chinese food and Linus. I screamed for my mom. Not for her to take me away or bring me anything. Just for her. I hadn't had a mom in so long.

In the back of my mind, I noticed a brick wall that had been in the white noise of my imagination ever since my parents died. When I screamed for my mom, it shook almost as if in answer.

I felt Jamie banging on the walls of my mind to let him in, but I held tight to my fortress so I could scream until I lost myself in the comfort of insanity.

Now I was dirty and unspecial with those filthy hands crawling all over me. I wanted to scream aloud and wipe them off me, but I couldn't move. So I called for my mom like a child and waited for her behind my closed eyelids.

18

DEALING

’m not sure how long it was before my eyes opened. My mother was holding me. Her arms were not repulsed by all the hands that had been on me. She did not turn away from my pain. Instead she snuggled me to her bosom and stroked my hair.

My body finally found itself and allowed me access to my tear ducts. I let myself go and cried into her dress. Movement told me she was crying too, and we were united in that. I found my arm and wrapped it around her, drawing comfort from the fact that she did not shirk away from how filthy I felt.

"There, there," she said, kissing my hair and holding me close. "We're alright. Nik got us out."

Nik? I pulled back and found not my mom, but Britta, her face soaked from tears. I sobbed all over again at the loss of my mother. Losing even the mirage of her was crushing, and I was already down for the count.

Britta kissed my temples and then called for her brother. "Jens! She's awake!"

Three seconds later, the door burst open. Jens looked like he had not slept in days. His hair was matted in parts and sticking up on its ends in the front. His clothes were rumpled and he had bags under his eyes, plus the bangs and bruises from killing the mountain trolls. "Lucy?"

In the next second, he was sitting up against the headboard between us, pulling me to his chest and propping up my limp frame with his strong one while his other arm banded around his sister. I meant to ask where we were, but my mouth was so dry; I couldn't make a sound without rasping.

Jens called over his shoulder, "I need water in here! Foss, get me some water!"

Britta combed her fingers through my tangles. "Lucy, sweetheart. You've been out three whole days! Tried everything to wake you!"

The expression on Jens's face broke my heart. "Awake, but not awake. Alive, but not. Don't do that! Don't shut down like that!" he yelled at me.

One day I was going to have to teach him how to talk to women.

A bare-chested Foss came in with water, but my hands were so weak from grief coupled with malnutrition that I couldn't hold the glass steady. Foss tipped the cup to my dry lips, and as my throat constricted, I winced at the effort it took. I could feel the hollow splash of the liquid as it hit my stomach and sloshed around the emptiness. The moment my throat found its use, I choked out, "I want my mom!"

There are most likely people who will look down on me for crying for my mommy. Those people did not have my mother. She could make a meal out of beans and a game out of an empty apartment. If she was here, surely she could fix the hands that felt seared on my body.

I turned into Jens and cried in his neck, my words muffled by his warm flesh. "I was pure! No one ever...and now I'm gross! I can feel their stupid hands still!"

He smoothed the hair back from my face too quickly to be soothing. "No, baby. You're not gross. You're perfect and special and everything... just everything. Foss and I tracked them down and killed nine of them. We'll find the others that did this to you and Britt. We'll tear their hands off so they never do this again. I've already got eighteen Nøkkendalig hands."

"I don't want to be here!" Then I gripped his shirt and let out a gut-curdling scream into his neck. "I don't want to feel this!"

"The marks will go away. We got you out in time. They're just light burns, and Alrik's cream'll take care of it in no time."

I pulled back and stared into his emerald eyes,

searching for something to force it all to make sense. "Marks?"

Jens shook his head. "Never mind." He held the hem of his shirt I was wearing down. "Don't worry about it right now."

Fear flared up in me, barely giving me a moment's respite. I tugged the hem up and saw large male handprints scattered around my torso.

I lost my mind. Despite the company, I ripped my shirt off and stared down at my chest covered only in my blue bra. My body was riddled with red handprints marking every spot that scarred my insides. I screamed and tried to claw them off my body. "No! Get them off me!" With every rake of my nails on my skin, the injuries burned anew as they had when I was underwater.

"Lucy, stop! Foss, help me!" Jens batted my hands away from my body, and then I felt Foss's arms fall around me from behind and squeeze, pinning my hands down at my sides.

And then I lost my shiz.

Foss was the last person I wanted near me. He was dangerous and hinted at my impending doom at the hands of his people. He was unsafe, and I was vulnerable. Plus, his breath smelled a little like vomit, and I could tell Mace had done another stripping of the curse while I was out. I flailed and kicked and thrashed around like a madwoman, crying and screaming for Foss to leave me alone.

"What the crap?" Jens tried to shush me, but it only

angered me further. "Foss, why's she so scared of you? Lucy, it's okay!"

"I don't know!" Foss yelled over my cries for help.

"Yes, you do! Yes, you do! You scared me on purpose, you horrible, awful man!"

I writhed and twisted in his arms, but all that managed to do was turn me so I was facing him. I wrenched my arms free, pushed at him and pounded with my fists on his massive chest, bawling for some freedom. We ended up wrestling on the floor when Foss could not keep me still, but I could not escape him fully.

"Stop it! I'm sorry!" Somehow without my knowledge or consent, Foss's hold mutated into a hard hug. He sat us up, palmed my back and held me to his chest, closing his eyes. "I'm sorry."

"No, you're not! You hate me! And I never did anything to you!" I struggled to leave the hug, but he was so much stronger than me.

"I'm sorry, Lucy!"

My fury broke into tears that poured over his shoulder, his hug turning my terror into mourning. "Get off me! Get the hands off me." I sobbed into his neck, despite myself. The only reason I can think that I cried on Foss's shoulder and allowed him to comfort me is that I was pretty insane at that point, and I couldn't escape him.

He shushed me like a parent calms a toddler and rocked me on his lap, rubbing my naked spine. He grabbed at the corner of the blanket that was on the bed behind me and pulled it down, draping it over my shoulders as his thumb continued to trace each of my ribs across my back.

Jens bent down and looked into my eyes, his expression almost as tortured as mine. "They'll fade away. Your body won't be marked forever."

I gave another small struggle in Foss's grip, but my heart wasn't in the escape anymore. His chest was warm against mine, and I sunk into it as my adrenaline ebbed. "Yes, it will." My voice dripped with the sadness that weighed my body down.

Foss spoke low in my ear. "We choose what marks us." His arm banded across my back in a show of protection and unified strength. "I'll find the others. The Nøkkendalig ends tonight." He spoke to me like he was swearing an oath of loyalty. "The Nøkkens are weak to've let them live this long." His voice lowered, the deep cadence tickling my ear. "But I am not weak."

I sagged in Foss's embrace. When we both decided I wasn't going to attack my own body anymore or his, he relaxed a little, allowing me to move my arms more freely.

I wound my arms around his thick neck and cried softly. "I want my mom. I just want my mom."

"I know, Lucy." His chin rested on my head. "I know. Me, too."

Then something brilliant clicked in my head. I turned my face from Foss's chest to peek at Jens. "I need to forget. Just for a little bit until I can deal. I can't handle this. It's crap on top of garbage on top of puke. It's too much." I swallowed hard and wiped a tear from my cheek. "That powder you have that makes you calm down. It takes away your pain."

Jens froze. "What about it?"

"I need it. I want it. I can't be alive like this. I can't... I just can't."

Foss, Jens and Britta all answered in a definitive "no."

I motioned to my marked body. "Look at me! I can't deal with this! I've been a halfway decent survivor until now. I need to not know any of this, even if it's just for a little while." I left Foss's protection and stood, wrapping my fingers in Jens's sweat-stained shirt. "Please, Jens. Just a little to take the edge off. I need something to keep me from feeling all this."

Jens shook his head, self-loathing etched all over his handsome face. "No, Loos. You can't handle this stuff. You have no idea how addictive it is or what it does to you really. You don't think I wish I'd never tried it? No. Don't check out. Don't get high. Don't shut yourself off and power down. Feel it. Feel all of it. I'm here, and I can help you. You're not alone this time."

I wanted to scream at him, "Yes, I am!" but tried a less mean approach. "Please, Jens," I whispered, nipping his lower lip.

"No."

Foss was livid. "Do it, and I'll shove your whole stash up your arse, Jens."

I kissed Jens lightly, pulling him closer. "Please."

His eyes closed, and I could feel his defenses melting. "I can't. You don't know what you're asking for."

"Please." I deepened the kiss, my tears wetting his lips.

Jens leapt back from me as if I'd singed him. "No, Loos! No!" He touched his lips and shook his head, pain and disgust mingling on his face. "Don't kiss me to take. Kiss me to give." His hurt was evident, and I shrank in my shame. "You're the only woman who's ever kissed me to give me something real. Every other girl wants to use me to up her status or get whatever money I've got. You're different. Don't be the same." He gave me a look that broke my heart all over again. "Don't ever do that to me again."

I whispered, "I'm sorry," and located the discarded shirt. I covered my body along with my shame and slumped onto the side of the bed. "Why don't you go? I'm crazy embarrassed right now. Like, nine kinds of crazy and seven kinds of embarrassed."

Jens chewed on his thumbnail. "Foss, could you and Britt give us a minute? And send in Henry Mancini."

Foss held out his hand. "Give me your stash first."

Jens glowered at him. "You act like I travel with it everywhere I go."

Foss stepped forward and yanked the cord from around Jens's neck, shoving the pouch in his pants pocket as he left. "I know a junkie when I see one. I'll be taking this."

"Screw you, Foss! It's your people the powder comes from." Jens called after him as Foss took Britta to the living room. He escorted her like she was a fragile old woman. Gentle, slow, and like he was transporting a great treasure. Even through my overly emotional craze, I couldn't help but marvel at the progress Mace was making in peeling back the layers of the Fossegrimen curse.

I waved my hand toward the door. "Just go, Jens. I'm fine if we're fine."

"Good to hear you're still full of it." He looked around the room as if trying to find something to adjust his stress level. He kicked off his boots and flopped on the bed, stretching his long form out. "Take a load off. Keep me company in this big empty bed. I've been out all night slaying dragons and whatnot."

Henry Mancini came scampering into the room and hopped up on the bed next to Jens, wagging his tail at me expectantly.

"I wish I was sure you were joking about the dragons. It feels like there's a new kind of terrible around every corner." I sighed, giving up my fight and lying down next to him. Henry Mancini licked my hand, and then laid down next to me so I was sandwiched in the middle. I traced loops and circles on Jens' stomach and chest. It relaxed me to calm him. I felt my anxiety dulling its sharp, unmerciful dagger as Henry Mancini cuddled into me from behind. "I'm sorry I kissed you like that. I was a little desperate."

"That's how I like my women. Good and desperate." He moved his arm under me and cradled my head in his nook.

He looked up at the wooden ceiling before speaking. "You know, I was pretty close with your family. Your parents knew how unhappy I was back home. When you and Linus were secure, every now and then your dad would take me out for a drink, and we'd talk about what we'd change if we could. We played darts, pool, or we'd just sit and talk. Point is, he was a decent guy. Towards the end, he guessed I had a little thing for you."

"You talked to my dad about me? Pretty ballsy."

Jens grinned. "That's me. I'm all kinds of ballsy." He brought his fingers up to brush through my blonde that was now stringy and dirty. "Linus knew first. He had a sixth sense when guys looked at you with Romeo eyes. Could even tell when I was invisible. I'm not ashamed to admit that I let the air out of a few tires of your secret admirers when I was looking after you."

"You evil mastermind," I joked, snuggling closer to his side.

"After they died, I was in pretty bad shape, too. They'd become like a family to me, especially after losing my parents to Be. You pulled one of these like you did today. Just checked right out after Alrik left. Laid on the floor of that apartment on Fifth, practically comatose. I tried a few things to snap you out of it without compromising my cover, but nothing worked." He pressed a kiss to my forehead, and his voice grew quiet. "There were a few nights that I covered you with a blanket and held you on the floor. I'm not ashamed to admit that I needed you then."

He kissed my lips, gentle and slow, like he was approaching a great treasure. "I need you now, too, Loos. When something too much happens, you can't check out like this. I've waited too long to be with you. So let me be there for you."

The burdens of my life that had been piled on my chest slowly began to lighten with the hope that I would not have to carry my grief alone. "I miss Linus," I admitted. "Sometimes I feel like no one'll ever understand me like that again. Like my whole life wasn't real because no one's around who remembers it."

Jens rolled on his side and pressed me into him, bringing the blanket up around us to create a cozy cave for my confessional. "I'm listening."

For some reason, those two simple words set something loose in my stalwart psyche. My misery began to tumble out of my mouth in words I had never been able to find before. Jens held me and listened, rubbing my back if I started to lose my hold on reality.

We'd been enemies. We'd been travel buddies. We'd been in serious like with each other, and maybe even love. But that day we became the best of friends. I spilled my grief, and then he finally let me in on his life, which I'd been kept far away from the details of.

"When your parents leave you on purpose, knowing the village is going to crap because of the trolls, it sucks. They went to the Land of Be and never thought twice of staying when Britt and I told them we wanted to stay."

"You seem pretty firm on that. You were never tempted?" I asked.

"Give up my arm and my freedom and myself all to just lay around and forget my life? No, thanks. Especially with how Pesta puts our souls to her use. I'm no one's bitch." He scrutinized my eyes. "Well, maybe yours."

"Aw. I've always wanted my very own bitch." I bowed my head like a queen. "You may keep both your arms."

He kissed my lips, like he'd forgotten the feel of how good we were together. "Thanks, babe." Our legs tangled through each other's as he further opened his vault. "Then I had to kill those trolls. People act like it's a huge deal, but it's not. No one wanted to be bothered, just like here with the Nøkkendalig. They'd rather give up their lives and leave for Be than stay and fight for what's theirs."

"But you love a good fight."

"Yes. And for a pacifist, so do you." He placed his hand on my hip and lightly stroked the skin there – a feather touching glass. "The cash reward was nice, but everyone changed. People I'd known for years treated me like I was untouchable. Girls who never gave me the time of day started throwing themselves at me. Nice for a minute, but it got old real fast. Nothing was real. Then the king started getting afraid for his throne. There was this song some girls made up that caught on and really set him off."

"Oh! Sing me the song." I lightly tugged on his shirt like a petulant child.

Jens grimaced. "Obviously not. This is story time, not song time."

"Was it about your animated eyebrows?"

Jens barked out a laugh at my unexpected guess. "Why would the king be jealous of that?" He waggled his black eyebrows at me. Henry Mancini was wary of the movement and cuddled into my back to warm me.

"Well, some people over-pluck theirs and never get them back. Maybe he's up at night penciling his in, thinking to himself he'll never have what it takes to cast emotion with his eyebrows the way the great Jens does."

"If you can believe it, you're the first woman to be taken with my eyebrows."

"That can't be true. Hmm. Was the song about your giant man muscles?" I lowered my voice to sound like a big man.

He flexed for my enjoyment. "This one? This mighty skull-crusher?"

"You name your biceps?"

"I do now. This one's called skull-crusher." He motioned to the one cradling my body. "What do you think the other should be called?"

Without considering better options, I blurted out the first thing that came to mind. "Jemima. Now, sing me that song."

"Oh, shut up. You can ask Jamie or Britt to sing it for you someday. Just make sure I'm far away." Jens kissed me again, making my toes arch. Henry Mancini yapped at us, breaking us apart. "Jemima. You're something else."

"It's done. It's named. I can't take it back."

He reached skull-crusher around me to pet Henry Mancini, caging me in with his arms. I dragged my fingernails through his hair, loving the look of his dark eyelashes fluttering shut as he enjoyed the simple touch. "Man, you own me when you do that." He studied my face for signs of stress at being so thoroughly contained in his arms. "Am I a safe place for you?"

I nodded, kissing him with the slow art we were becoming adept at. "I think you might be my only safe place in Undraland. How about we stop fighting so much and start taking care of each other better?"

Jens gave in to my invitation, running his arm down my hip and cupping the underside of my thigh so he could move it closer. "You got it, Mox."

Henry Mancini snuggled into my back, contentedly listening to us kiss and laugh as we deepened our connection.

19

SAFETY WITH OLIN AND OLINA

Given Nik's hero status amongst his people, and the fact he was in his thirties, it was strange to me that he still lived with his parents. His mother was prone to gushing about lace doilies, and his father was only missing a pipe to complete the 1950s vibe he had going.

That night, his mother cooked a roast over the fire and brought it in for "Niklas's little friends." She acted like we were having a slumber party, and she was just happy her son had friends. I could smell desperation when she asked me if I was married.

"Mother!" Nik cautioned. "Queen Lucy is just a friend." He cast me an apologetic look as he offered me another roll.

I sat up straighter and chewed the meat in my mouth with a more ladylike air at mention of my fake royalty.

"Hmm? Oh, yeah. Wish I could, but I can't marry your son. Got a world to run and all that. Wow, this roast is delicious."

"Are you seeing anyone, dear?" the woman prodded, still campaigning pretty hard for her son. "My Niklas is a hero to the Nøkken, you know. He rid our village of a troll infestation not too long ago."

"You don't say." I grinned at Nik from across the table, who shot me a warning look. "I actually am seeing someone." Jens stepped on my foot to let me know not to say it was him. "King Ian Somerhalder. Beautiful man."

Jens tried to cover his snort with a cough. "Sorry. Could I get another roll, Nik?"

"All out." Nik picked up the empty basket as proof.

His mother took the basket and stood. She wore a formal ball gown at the table, surrounded by a bunch of vagrants. "I'll get some more. Olin, would you help me bring out the dessert? The tray's a little heavy."

"Of course, Olina."

Olin and Olina. Totally cute.

As soon as the parental units were gone, Jens took a drink, casting me half a glance. "I could take Ian Somerhalder." He was probably not the first boyfriend who felt inferior at mention of the sexiest vampire actor ever.

"Hello, he's a vampire."

Jens set down his cup and rolled his eyes. "I love that you think the real Ian Somerhalder is an actual vampire."

"Of course he is. No one's that good an actor." I took

another bite of the garlic-laden roast. "Why can't I say I'm with you? Keeping your options open for Nik?" I winked at Nik, who winked at Jens.

Jens responded by seductively licking his bite of meat in Nik's direction. "Yes, that's exactly it. No, babe. You're a queen to them. If you were with me, it would make you more common in their eyes. Best keep you untouchable. I'm your Tom, and you're my charge."

"Oh, you with the romantic talk. You sure know how to make a girl blush. 'Charge' is code for something saucy, right?"

"Yes. I say you're my charge, but I'm really calling you the pain in my ass." Jens addressed Jamie's wistful smile directed at us. "What?"

Jamie shrugged. "Nothing. It's just nice to see you like this. You're happy. Never thought it would happen for you. You've always been a little surly."

"Whatever. I'm a joy."

"Yes." I kissed Jen's temple. "'Joy' is code for 'big, giant grump.'"

He grumbled under his breath, proving my point. "Don't get me wrong. I love the family feel, Nik, but we're going to need a little space to plan your part in all this."

Nik cut his meat like a gentleman next to Tor, who shoveled the mutton down his pie hole without the use of utensils that would only slow him down.

It was then I noticed Britta was pushing her food around on her plate without really eating. She looked how

I felt before Jens calmed me down, and a little how I still felt. She had a burned handprint on her cheek – a constant reminder of the assault. Though it would heal, I knew her insides would take longer to rid themselves of her many scars.

The thing that bothered me about it was that Jamie still kept a friendly distance from her. In between bites, Jens would reach out and rub my knee under the table. My foot was nudged up against his, savoring the small assurances that we were good together, and I wasn't alone in my pain. I observed Jamie pretending that he was not madly in love with Britta, and that her torture did not torment him.

"Mom, Queen Lucy has official business to speak to us about in private. Could we take our desserts to the parlor?"

"Of course, Niklas. You go have your important meeting with your big important friends." She clasped her hands together. "Oh! My son, King of the Other Side!"

"Mom!" Nik protested, shaking his head in apology to me as we all stood. I thanked her for the meal, and then we headed down the hallway.

Jens wound his fingers through mine. "You can't even hold onto Ian Somerhalder in your pretend life. You've already been auctioned off to Nik."

"I could do worse," I reasoned, sizing up the tall man with sparkly white and blue hair. "Imagine how our kids would look. My height with his fluffy hair? Stellar. A family of mini Einsteins."

"I've seen your baby pictures. You'll have cute kids no matter what." He kissed my temple, warming me from the inside out. The more we learned to work together, the more he exuded comfort. I lapped up his sunshine like it was my last day on earth, cozying into his side as we walked. I guessed it would be inappropriate to jump his bones in the middle of the hallway, but the idea did cross my mind.

Then I saw Jamie walking a respectable distance behind Britta, and the image broke me from my bliss. "Give me a minute." Then I addressed my laplanded buddy. "Hold up, Jamie. I need to talk to you."

Jamie looked surprised, but indulged me. We hung behind while the others went into the room ahead. "Is everything alright?"

I shook my head. "Look, we all know you and Britta have a thing going. You hid it in front of Nik's parents, but when it's just our group? Girlfriend's falling apart over there, and you're worried about social propriety? I don't get it. She needs you!" I looked up at him with a hint of scolding in my eyes.

Jamie exhaled. "The Tomten aren't like you humans. Maybe it's normal for you to make your love public, but it's not for us unless we're married. We both know that can never be. She's been through enough. I won't put her through a social shaming."

I motioned around the wooden walls bedecked with frilly artwork and knitted knickknacks. "You call this public? It's just us in here. This whole time in the mountains? Who are the rocks going to tell? You're being stupid. She's just been through the smack of it in that river, and you're keeping her from the one thing that'll help. Maybe you won't have her forever, but this trip is your one chance to have what both of you always wanted. You have a limited amount of time together, and you're wasting it pretending like we won't approve of the thing we all know should be happening." I pointed to the room. "Now go in there and make yourself useful. Do you think she can handle what just happened to her?"

Jamie's face shifted. His eyes were wide, looking slightly unhinged. "Do you think *I* can handle what happened to her? To you?" He rolled up the hem of his shirt, exposing the handprints that burned themselves into his skin via our psychic link. I gasped, flinching at the sight. "I'm sick just thinking about it!"

"Then do something about it!" I countered. "Jens killed the smackholes that did this to us, and then he held me until I came back to myself. You need her, and she needs you. She didn't sign on for all this. She came for you!"

Jamie held up his hands and backed up, taking a deep breath. "I don't want to hurt her when we get back and I have to marry Freya."

"So instead you're hurting her now? Be alive for once in your life." I crossed my arms over my scarred chest. "And you can stop pretending that you'll go through with that betrothal. I'm taking you over to the Other Side when it's time to destroy the last portal, and you're not coming back."

Jamie gave a short, perfunctory laugh laced with bitterness. "You act like it's all so simple."

"It is." I nodded once. "I'm the Queen, and I command it so."

He covered his face with his hands. "I wish I could be hopeful, like you."

I reached up and pried his hands from his face. "You're crazy in love with Britta. Whatever it takes, I'll make this happen for you. You just have to stop being such a wuss. Not sexy."

Jamie's cheeks reddened. "I'm not sure I would fit in on your side. I will never get used to a woman talking like that."

"Man up, chief." I chucked him in the arm. "We're stuck with each other, so you might as well get used to it."

We entered the parlor together, with Jens shooting me an inquisitive eyebrow arch. I friggin' loved his eyebrows. So expressive. I waved off his unspoken questions.

Uncle Rick called the room to order, and I noticed Mace by his side. He'd been missing at dinner. He had a resigned look on his face and bags under his eyes. I moved across the room and stood next to him, bumping my hip to his side. He offered up a half-smile and poked me in the back with his prehensile cow's tail. I really hoped I'd get used to that one day.

Uncle Rick cleared his throat. "I think the best time to

move forward is after we've all had a couple good nights of sleep. We're not suspected to be here, and I've already spoken to Olin and Olina. They've agreed to keep our visit a secret for now."

I cast Jens a disbelieving look. Nik's mom wouldn't be able to keep quiet for long. She was practically over the moon that a Queen was staying in her house and would hopefully marry her son. I could already hear the gossip mill turning.

Jens raised two fingers to interrupt. "I agree, but let's keep it to one more night here. I don't like the idea of staying in one place for long. Eventually word'll spread this way. I'd like to be gone long before then."

Uncle Rick spread out his palms. "Any objections to setting about our deed tomorrow? It's another four days' journey to the portal, and I think we could use some respite if we're to resist more of the Nøkken song."

20

SOMETHING TO TALK ABOUT

When night fell, Nik sang a song to help everyone make good use of their time spent sleeping. I sat curled up in Jens's lap in the parlor with everyone else. When the song began, we were holding hands, my back to his chest, looking wistfully at Nik as he lulled us all.

Nik was beautiful when he sang. The shimmer in his fluffy hair was a gentle brush of magic that added to the ambiance. A fire roared in the hearth, crackling almost in rhythm with his melody. My heart hurt when he reached the high notes, and I finally understood why people loved the opera so much, not that his voice was strictly operatic. It was lovely, and so was he.

Foss started snoring on the rug, with Henry Mancini resting his snout on his tattooed forearm. Tor was grumbling something in his sleep. Uncle Rick and Charles rested on their mats, the worries of both worlds off their shoulders for those few hours of respite. Jamie actually took my advice and cuddled up next to Britta, the firelight dancing off their knit-together bodies with elegance that took my breath away.

Jens. Stunning Jens. I needed, wanted and appreciated him with equal intensity. His thick black eyelashes that were just wasted on a man swept his cheekbones and made him, if possible, more enthralling to watch. He breathed, and I breathed, and for all its wrongness, the world felt right.

When the song ended, everyone in the room was asleep, except for Nik and me.

"Whoa! That's crazy, Nik," I whispered. I pecked Jens's cheek and detached myself from his lax embrace. Nik hoisted me up and led me into the kitchen, where he made me a cup of tea by candlelight. We sat at the lace-covered table and blew on our hot beverages, enjoying the peace of civilized company.

"How are you, darling?" Nik asked, studying my face for signs of a lie.

"Your parents' place is amazing. It's like the mid-twentieth century in here, minus electricity. How'd that happen?"

"Pirates."

"Come again? Like, yo ho mateys?" I did my best impression, but I was kinda tired, so it fell flat.

"Huh? *Pirates*," he repeated, as if I hadn't heard him

correctly the first time. "Nøkken and Fossegrimens who go over to the Other Side and bring back treasure."

"Seriously? So that's where all this came from. Weird. Is that kosher?"

"If you mean legal, not anymore. It's a practice that policies have been put up against so it doesn't happen as much. Undrans don't want to cross over, now that the Huldra are running loose on your side. I would imagine these are quite outdated. My parents acquired them before I was born."

"Well, it's lovely. How are you after giving up your secret about Bjorn and all that?"

Nik looked into his cup like he was hoping it held a pit big enough for him to hide in. "I feel small, surrounded by giants. Much how you must feel physically, I'd imagine."

"You were big yesterday. You saved my life and Britta's."

Nik offered a wan smile. "Yes, a real hero. All I managed to do was get you both out. Mace sucked the water from your lungs. Jens and Foss killed the Nøkkendalig – a thing my entire people have been too afraid to attempt."

"Hey, now. You rescued me. You led the rescue team that saved Queen Lucy of the Other Side. That'll make a good headline, for sure."

He sipped his tea as the candlelight danced on his sunkissed skin. "You're too kind."

"The one time you can actually brag, and you're being too modest. I don't get it."

"Soon I'll become the biggest criminal in Nøkken history. Worse than the Nøkkendalig. I'll be hated and my parents shamed in front of the country. Forget Bjorn and rescuing you. *That* will be my legacy." He held his teacup up in salute. "Well, it was nice while it lasted."

I placed my hand on his. "That's assuming you get caught, which if all goes well, you won't."

Nik smiled at me in that way parents get when teenagers start talking about the problems in the world and how they can be fixed. "The Nøkken portal is deep underwater. There's no way a Tomten can vanish me that far and live to tell the tale. It will be guarded, for certain. I've thought it through." He sipped his tea. "There's no way I won't be found out. I've made my choice, and I'm okay with it. I'll be sentenced and executed, and that's the way of it."

I rested my toes on his. "I know why Jens and a few of them feel the way they do about Be. But what makes you so certain it's an evil place worth getting executed for?"

Nik avoided my eyes as if looking into them might reveal his secrets. "I lost a friend to Be. A dear one." He kept staring into his cup. "Kirk."

"Ah." I nodded in understanding, recalling the times I'd noticed Nik checking out Jens's stellar backside. "I'm guessing your world isn't as accepting of your 'friendship' with Kirk as you'd like, huh."

"We don't speak of it. We were young, teenagers, and

his parents found out. They sent him to Be to hide their shame."

My mouth fell open, and I'm surprised a slew of four-letter words didn't come flying out. "Can people do that? Force someone into Be?"

"In the end, it has to be their decision, but there was not much choice in the matter. So Kirk is gone, and I am alone. I wandered in the mountains often to have space for my grieving. That's how I met Bjorn. He's been a great comfort to me through the years. As you can see, I'm well past marrying age, and people are starting to talk." He took a sip, his eyes turning steely. "When Alrik presented me with his plan, I did not hesitate, and I will not hesitate tomorrow when it's time to end the gateway that took my... myself away from me. Pesta will pay, and I'm glad to be part of that."

I let his anger settle for a moment before speaking. "Well, you'll be happy to hear that the world evolves. People change. Maybe not soon, but it does happen. Used to be like that in my world. Still is in some places."

"Used to?"

"Not so much anymore. In a lot of places, men can even marry each other."

He set his teacup down in shock. "That's not possible. Society would never allow it."

"There's always going to be those people who treat others in ways they'll regret in twenty years, but they're everywhere. But yeah, it's possible. Legal. In some places it's totally normal."

Nik gripped the table and stared at me with such intensity, I was nervous he might shout when he opened his mouth. "Are you telling me the absolute truth?"

I cocked my head to the side. "Why would I lie about that? Of course it's true."

He leaned over the table, grabbed my face and kissed me square on the mouth before I had a moment to protest. He held his face inches from mine and stared into my eyes with bold determination. "We *have* to find a way for me to live through this and see your side. I don't care what it takes. I'll do anything. I just need to know it's possible. That people like me can be happy."

He released me, and I flopped back on my chair, flabbergasted. "I thought that was the plan anyway, so that works for me."

"Lucy, you are fair, that's for certain. Jens is a lucky man."

I drained the last of my tea and stood, holding my hand out to him. "Gossip's really that bad around here?"

Nik nodded with disappointment painting his eyes as he took my hand. "Bad enough for parents to send their children to a soulless eternity if they disgrace the family name."

"Then let's give the locals something to talk about." I pulled him to standing. "I'm beat. Let's see how your mom freaks out in the morning when we come out of the same room. How fast do you want to bet that spreads around town?"

Nik was taken aback by my daring. "Are you serious? What about Jens?"

"He'll understand. I'll have to tell him about Kirk, but he can keep it to himself."

"Are you sure about this?" He towered over me, sizing up my commitment as I nodded.

"Sure. But for the record, I was amazing in the sack. You could barely keep up with my double-jointed flexible human female ways."

He held up his hand in promise. "I will look appropriately exhausted by your acrobatics in the morning."

"Oh! First things first. Do you have any shaving cream?" Yeah, that was a non sequitur.

"Um, yes. Why?"

"I owe Foss a little payback. He's out cold, right?"

Nik retrieved the shaving cream, and I plopped a dollop in Foss's outstretched hand. Let that teach him to be a jerk to me.

Nik hefted me over his shoulder like a caveman, spilling my giggles all over the place as he stalked past his parents' bedroom to his. Their door cracked open, and I knew the gossip mill would be grinding out the good stuff before noon.

Nik dropped me onto his bed and we chatted in whispers as we prepared for some much needed sleep. We lay next to each other, comparing our worlds and laughing at the differences. When the laughter turned to yawns, Nik kissed my forehead. "I think it's time we actually slept together."

I rolled onto my side facing away from him and felt his body shift next to mine. "Nik, could you sing me to sleep? I know your magic doesn't work on me, but I really like the sound of it."

His smile was evident in his tone as he brushed his fingers through my long hair. "As you wish, darling. Sleep well, my queen."

Nik sang to me soft songs telling the history of great Nøkken heroes and their daring feats. His voice was warm chocolate melting over my body. Then he paused, and the key shifted to a minor tune, his volume quieting as if sharing a secret of great import to him.

One day, long ago the fear of trolls filled the globe.

But children play and women sing because the Nøkken triumphs ring.

Man of Valor, that's our Nik. When he walks by, our hearts beat quick.

Men and women, much we owe. We bow to Nik, true Nøkken hero.

There was a sadness to his voice as he sang the tune filled with slow, sad notes that were meant to be joyful. "Nik," I whispered, reaching my arm behind me to brush his cheek with the back of my knuckles. "Thank you for saving my life."

He caught my fingers and kissed each tip. It would've

been sexy if I wasn't head over heels for Jens, and if Nik wasn't, well, gay.

I rolled onto my back and brought his head to my chest so I could stroke his fluffy hair. I'd never pet anything so soft, even Henry Mancini. Nik continued singing as he pulled the covers up over us.

I closed my eyes, and though there was no magic to it, I drifted off to sleep with my true Nøkken hero resting in my arms.

21

BEWITCHED BY CHARLES

"So that was a neat little trick with the shaving cream," Foss said, his expression surly as ever. I was beginning to wonder how thin the layers of curse were that Mace was peeling back. Granted, he hadn't choked me since, but he was a long way from Ward Cleaver.

"Glad you liked it." I'd heard his defamatory exclamations when he awoke with the white cream smeared all over his hand, face and hair. It brought me no uncertain amount of joy to get his goat. "Think of it as one prank for every time you called me and Britt little rats."

Just as I got my porridge perfectly seasoned with cinnamon and sugar, Foss reached out his large mitt, cupped the back of my head and shoved my face down into my breakfast. "That's one payback for every time I've regretted going on a journey with women slowing us down."

Charles and Jamie made exclamations of protest, but Jens knew better. He sat back, an ankle resting atop his knee and a lazy smile on his face as he ate his porridge.

I wiped the oats off my face, grinning at the game that had been unleashed. This would be fun.

Before we set out on our trek along the outskirts of Nøkken, Charles and Nik put as much protection on us as they could in the privacy of the parlor. Nik sang a song to increase our energy and focus. Charles unleashed his bizarre several-noted whistle I still could not make sense of, explaining that it would help us work in better spirits with each other and open us up to new ideas that might show us a way to get Nik out without getting caught.

Then Charles pulled me to my feet, held onto my hand and whistled in almost a whisper. My ear gravitated toward his mouth just as it had the first time he'd enchanted me so. I had no idea what it would do, but my body drank in the different pitches and savored every note that bent my mind to his will. His lips caressed and puckered on my ear, lulling me into whatever trance he wished for me. He had one hand around my hips and the other cupping my chin. I felt completely secure, my body oddly boneless.

When Mace released me, Jens snatched me back, shattering my drugged haze. He'd been on and off grouchy since I informed him of why I slept with Nik. He understood, but I could tell he was unhappy about it. "Don't do that to her without telling me what it's for, Mace. She's my girlfriend, not yours. Plus, she's my charge. I should know how she's being toyed with."

"Toyed with? You sound like a jealous fool," Mace replied, unfazed at Jens's mood. To be fair, Jens was always in a mood.

"How would it sound if I punched you in the face?" Jens challenged.

Mace looked around the room, incredulous. "It would sound like you're a jealous fool! Am I saying it wrong?"

I moved between the two oxen and pressed a hand to both their chests. I kissed Mace's cheek and said to him, "You're my brother. Quit winding up my guy." Then I turned to Jens and said, "You really think I'm going to leave you for my brother? Quit being weird." Then I licked the side of his face from chin to temple. He was not amused, but my spirits were soaring out of nowhere.

My intervention wasn't as helpful as I was hoping, but at least they fumed silently after that. I was too excited to see the land of Nøkken to care.

Nik's mother brought me extra pears after breakfast and made sure I had too many apples stuffed in my pack for the journey ahead. We told her Nik was showing us all around Nøkken. She was so thrilled that her son had a prestigious prospect that she did not question the lie. "You're just an absolute doll!" I exclaimed, pinching the woman's cheeks. My head felt like it was floating, and everything was funny, including Foss, who was never funny.

I tied the laces of his rugged leather boots in quadruple knots, laughing hysterically when he moved to put them on and could not. His frown was hilarious to me, so the more he used it, the funnier it became. I was outright cackling by the time we left.

We set out for our grand Nøkken adventure early in the morning. Uncle Rick and Charles separated from the group to venture into the main city to purchase more supplies. The rendezvous point was two whole days' journey away.

Henry Mancini went nuts at the innumerable amount of giant multicolored birds that fluttered around in the air. It was early autumn, but other than the crisp breeze that had an undercurrent of warmth to it, nature around us was burgeoning spring. Tulips bloomed everywhere in the boldest colors so vivid, you would swear they were painted. Some appeared tie-dyed, growing straight out of the ground. There were lilies and enormous snapdragons that stretched almost as tall as small trees, bending every which way with the wind. One of the snapdragon mouths fell open, and I laughed when I realized I could fit my entire head inside. There were tropical birds and average Midwest birds and giant feathered friends I'd never heard of before. Some of them sang songs that were so beautiful, I felt lighter than a feather as I scampered along after my puppy.

Since we were walking on the outskirts of Nøkken, we didn't see many homes. The locals we saw were only in the distance, but I could hear them.

The song of the Nøkken was crazy. Since I wasn't from Undraland, it had no effect on me, other than sounding pretty. I mean, some of the most engaging voices I'd ever heard. Move over, Auto-tunes. Double melodies coming from one mouth, trilling and beckoning for all they were worth. Nik had to sing much of the way just to keep our crew from following after the airy tunes.

I could tell Jens wanted to be grouchy, but I was too happy to let that fly. Colors were a beautiful thing. After being surrounded by mountains that were gray, gray and more gray, it was a breath of luscious air to be smacked in the face with Technicolor.

I raced Henry Mancini until my heart pounded with elation. I was not climbing harrowing heights. There were no softball-sized venomous spiders. The Nøkkendalig were pretty well obliterated, and I had my regular clothes back that Nik's mom had washed during the night.

I pumped my legs, laughing at the ease with which Henry Mancini beat me. We ran, just me and my dog, until my head started to throb. I turned and found the others much farther back than I anticipated. Jamie was laughing, a nice big belly one that rang out across the prairie. Jens was trotting in my direction, his face too adult and serious for my liking.

Jens waved his arms to flag me down. "Didn't you hear me? I've been calling for you to slow down."

"I can't!" I answered, my heart racing. "I'm too happy. This place is gorgeous! Can we live here when it's all over?"

"No. Get back here!" Jens yelled. "You're giving yourself a headache."

"I don't care!" I shouted back, running with Henry Mancini. I tripped and fell in the grass, rolling around in the green with the dog I always wanted.

When Jens trotted toward me, I was ready. Grin as wide as my face, I stood and jumped up on him, wrapping my legs around his waist and kissing his surprised mouth like I never had before. I devoured him, pulling his hair and squeezing with my thighs. He was so taken aback that he lost his balance and fell on his backside, taking me down with him.

This did not deter me. I mean, I'm the girl who stole her teacher's car and parked it at a strip club for calling my brother "chemo boy", so I can be pretty determined. I pushed Jens further into the tall grass and kissed him over and over. His protests melted under my fervor until I tried to take his shirt off.

"Wait, Lucy! Stop for a second."

I pulled back from his lips and delivered a loud raspberry to his toned stomach, making him jerk in surprise. I contented myself burying my nose in his belly button and biting the skin beneath lightly. Henry Mancini barked at us, which for no reason at all was the funniest sound I ever heard.

"Oh! You know what we should do? We should get Indian food from that killer place in Indiana. Indian food in Indiana! Ha! Remember that? And then I could eat it off your face like this." I straddled his chest and mimed eating buckets of Spicy Rogan Josh off his face with my hands. "Curried Jens. Delish!"

"Lucy, what's your deal?"

"My deal? I'm so happy! And I think we should celebrate. Right here." I planted a rough kiss on his lips to stifle his protest. "Oh, man! You taste good even without the curry."

"You know they can see us, right?" Jens tried to resist me, but I was on high octane.

"Then they're gonna get a good show."

I heard Jamie's barking laugh, uninhibited by his station or propriety, followed by Britta's astonished gasp. "James! You can't do that out here!"

"Why? Why not? Why can't I kiss the woman I love? I'm filled with the stuff. Absolutely exploding with love for the most beautiful Tomten alive!" he shouted, declaring his love for all of nature to hear.

"Jamie! What's gotten into you?" Britta pushed him away, her blush visible even from a distance.

"You have!" He tapped his forearms. "You're in my veins! Every beat of my lonely heart sings for you! Every night, I go to bed thinking about you, and each morning, I get out of bed only for the hope of seeing your face."

She gasped, straightening her bonnet that he began unlacing. "You can't speak of such things! What about Freya? You're promised to another woman and you're laplanded to Lucy. You can't possibly begin to tell me how this could work."

Jamie held up his hands to the Heavens, a new man coming from the baptism of whatever set me off. "I renounce my claim on the Tonttu throne! I renounce my title, my status and my father!"

Foss, Tor, Nik and even Jens stopped to stare in shock at Jamie, who looked more alive than he ever had been. His grin was bursting off his face, chest barreled and life – real life filled every pore of his body. He was a new man...

...on bended knee. "Britta, will you marry me? Most wonderful woman I've ever known. Be my bride!"

Britta stumbled back into Nik, who barely had enough wits about himself to right her. "What?" Foss, Nik, Britta and Jens exclaimed as one.

Jens dumped me off of him, which made me laugh. I pumped my fist in the air. "You do it, Jamie! You get your girl!" Then to the sky I belted out a triumphant, "Carpe diem!"

Jens was on his feet, eyes wide and hand over his mouth as he witnessed what he thought he would never see. His sister wept as she nodded her answer.

Jamie was a rocket that only needed Britta to launch

him into outer space. He leapt to his feet only to tackle her to the ground, rolling around in the grass with abandon. Britta's bonnet fell off, and he marveled at the dark braids he had been yearning for since he met her.

Britta allowed herself to be kissed in public. Granted, there was only the seven of us plus Henry Mancini, but it was a big leap for her.

Jamie's sudden spring of lust ricocheted to me, bouncing through my veins like a pinball machine. Everything carnal within me flared up, a fire on my insides ripping desire through every artery. I stood, zeroing in on Jens, whose back was to me.

He turned in slow motion, in shock over his sister and best friend making out in the grass, now affianced. "Can you believe that?" he said, flabbergasted.

It was the sexiest thing I'd ever heard him say, but I couldn't tell you why. I jumped up on him again, mashing my lips to his. "I want to paint your body with these tulips."

"What the... Loos!" He turned his head after a solid minute of sating my need for him. "Shh. Maybe you should give my two lips a rest for a second." He gently extracted me from his body, chest heaving as he sized me up. "What's gotten into you?"

I twirled around like I used to when I was a little girl until I got so dizzy, I fell. I rolled over onto my back, spreading out my limbs in the green. "I'm in love! My heart's so happy, I feel like I'm gonna burst with fruit flavor!" I acted out what it would look like if my chest opened up and my heart floated out and exploded all over creation. I'd seen enough zombie movies to do an accurate rendition of the gore. My sound effects were pretty spot on.

"Nik!" Jens called. Foss and Nik ran toward him, way too serious for my liking. "What did you do, Nik? Did you addle her brains with your songs?"

Nik looked down on my giddy grin in confusion. "Nøkken songs don't work on her. You know that. Besides, I didn't sing anything that would make her ecstatic like this." He looked around, listening to the other songs that stretched to us. "No one else is, either."

"Anything that would make Jamie lose his mind? Or maybe just his inhibitions?" Foss questioned. "They're laplanded. Maybe it's affecting her through him."

Nik trotted away from my cackling to listen closer to the songs in the distance. "I'm telling you, there's nothing that would do this to Jamie. It's all just songs for peaceful thinking, bountiful crops and things of that sort."

Jens ran his hands through his tousled hair, his wide eyes watching me do the backstroke in the grass. "Something's wrong. She's cracked. I've never seen her like this before."

Foss, Nik and Jens all bent over me to observe with caution, but I couldn't stop laughing. When I noticed a tiny streak of white shaving cream under Foss's jawbone, I laughed so hard, I started crying. I pointed, but was unable to hiccup out what it was that set me off. Even when Foss pushed my head into the grass to hold it still, I couldn't stop the hysterics. He pried open my eyes and snapped his fingers in my face, which only made me hoot louder.

Foss. Pretending to care like a doctor would. I'm telling you, anyone would find that hilarious.

"It's the Huldra whistle," Foss ruled. "Dilated pupils and hands like ice. Charles spelled us all back at Nik's house, but it's worn off on us." Foss pressed my hand to Jens's forearm so he could feel the difference in temperature between his warm one and my freezing one. "I guess she's just more susceptible to his magic."

They were all talking and acting worried, which added to my levity for no reason at all. A few minutes later, I was picked up and hoisted over Jens's shoulder. We moved forward toward the rendezvous point, but I could not have cared less. My hair bounced and dangled, the curls entertaining me the whole way.

22

"Okay, it was cute the first ten minutes, but I can't take much more of this. Where's Alrik?" Nik complained, looking out from behind a grassy hill that stretched seven stories high. It was one of dozens in this area, and made for a nice waiting spot.

It was dark out, and Jamie and I were lying in the grass on either side of Britta, looking up at the stars and laughing at the dirty shapes the bright dots made. Britta told us the story of one of the constellations before we lost focus and started making up our own "hilarious" versions. Most of them involved bowel movements at inappropriate times, which could not have made us laugh more. Britta was absolutely crimson, and had given up on shushing us long ago.

Jens was sharpening his knives on a stone while Foss gulped from his canteen, exhausted from carrying Jamie for the better part of a day. "You're too far away!" I complained to Jens with a giggle, rolling over onto my stomach and propping myself up on my elbows. "I miss you like a warm, fuzzy mitten, you handsome man! Come be my warm, fuzzy mitten." I gave him my best come hither eyes and my most dazzling grin.

Jens's smile returned to me wary. "Keep talking, nympho! I'm staying right here until you get some actual adult supervision."

Foss was flabbergasted when I blew Jens a kiss and then stage whispered some very unladylike things to him. He turned to Jens with admiration in his eyes. "You deserve some kind of medal for this. She's bent on you, but you're over here with a bunch of smelly men."

Jens clapped Foss on the back too hard to be genuine. "What can I say? You're a lovely bunch." He took a bite of his apple, looking at me like he wished he was by my side. "I can't go over there. If I do, I'll... you can tell she's not right in the head. I can't take advantage like that."

Nik chuckled from his lookout position. "You're a good man, Jens."

"Yeah. Lucky me. Where the smack is Alrik?" He looked up to the heavens in exasperation. "Great, Mox. Now you've got me saying it." He rubbed the back of his neck. "And why didn't she fall asleep last night with your song, Nik? She's laplanded to Jamie."

Nik shrugged. "You know sleep isn't connected between laplanders." He had tried singing a song to calm

Jamie down, but it didn't work on either of us. "Her hands are ice and her pupils are dilated. She's been bewitched by Mace. It's the only explanation. The Nøkken song is powerful, but it doesn't control people. It only suggests. Mace has to undo it."

I started reassembling the braids Jamie had taken out of Britta's hair with fingers that were trembling with jubilation. I could not help but kiss her cheek every few seconds. "I'm so happy for you!"

Jamie took the responsibility of smooching her other cheek in rhythm with me. "I'm so happy for me! Let's get married tonight, my love. This very night!"

"Why wait?" I agreed, high-fiving Jamie, our matching grins making Britta bury her face in her hands. "Oo! I've never been to a wedding before!"

We kept smooching her cheeks until Nik pulled me away. "You *are* a problem, aren't you? Worse than your wolf with all your energy."

"Oh, Nik! Isn't it all just so wonderful! Undraland is the most beautiful place I've ever seen! Nøkken is amazing. Except for all the rapists." I don't know why, but this made me laugh so hard, I doubled over on the ground. "Get it? Because rapists, they're not amazing! Ha!"

Jamie giggled into Britta's cheek. "I get it, Lucy! And now they're dead! Ha!"

Thankfully Uncle Rick and Mace turned up before we found anything worse to laugh about.

"You!" Jens called out through the night in accusation.

"What?" Mace sneered, taking a defensive step back.

"You did something to her in your whistle. I know you did. What did you make her feel? She's been out of her mind for two days now!"

Uncle Rick whirled on Charles after glancing at me. "What happened, son?"

"Nothing!" Mace's hands were raised in surrender.

Jens was in no mood. "What was the third whistle for? I know it was you."

Mace shrugged. "Oh, you know. Just general health and stuff."

Jens clenched his fists. "Are you trying to be a bad liar, or are you just trying to get me angry?"

Tor pushed his hand to Jens's chest to keep him from lunging. "Easy, boy."

Mace eyed Jens in challenge. "Maybe both at this point. Although, I really don't have to try to get you angry. Seems like existing does the trick well enough on its own."

Uncle Rick took one look at Jamie and me on the grass, checked my pupils, touched my hands and turned to Mace. "Undo it, young man. Your spell shouldn't have lasted this long. Most Huldras' wear off in a few hours."

I pointed and guffawed at my half-brother. "Uh-oh! He young-manned you, Mace! That can't be good."

Jamie pointed to the hill. "Go sit in the corner, young man!"

"Time out for you, young man!" I giggled on the grass even as Mace knelt next to me. "Get it? Because he's mad at you, and you're a boy! You're in trouble!" I teased, grinning up at him. "You know what else has tails like you? Comets! You have to help me find one!"

Charles smiled forlornly at me. "Look up at the stars, beautiful girl. Find my comet." Then he pulled me onto his lap while I giggled at the sky, searching for any sign of a comet to report and make my joke complete.

He pressed his lips to my ear, and more laughter bubbled out of me like a fountain filled with cola. "Uh-oh! You're kissing my ear again. Jens is not gonna be happy about that. Big trouble... *young man!*"

This set Jamie off in hysterics again.

Mace whistled a slow, steady note in my ear. At first, I was grinning so wide, I thought I might split my face. As the note progressed and mutated, my smile wilted. My eyes drooped as my muscles began to loosen from the tension built over the course of two days spent laughing. Before I knew it, my whole body was jelly, and I flopped back lifelessly in my brother's arms.

23

HUMILIATION AND HUBRIS

I awoke to a fire crackling I don't know how many hours later. I opened my heavy lids and saw four skinned kanins roasting over the spit. Jens's back was to me, and his arm was around his sister, who was staring with a far-off expression into the flames. I was on the grass next to a snoozing Jamie, alerting no one of my awaking.

"Are you going to be okay?" Jens asked quietly. "I'm sorry you were proposed to like that. It's not fair to either of you."

Britta offered her brother a soft smile. "I never thought Jamie would ever ask me to marry him. It was a dream come true. Even if it has to go back to just being a dream, I'm glad it happened."

Jens kissed her forehead. "You know he would if he could."

"I do now," she said, wiping a tear from her eye. "It's fine, Jens. It was a beautiful dream, and I don't regret having it, however brief." She nudged his ribs. "It must have been nice to have Lucy so taken with you."

I caught a glimpse of Jens's grin. That gorgeous mouth I so often wanted to both smack and kiss was every bit as alluring as it had ever been. "It's always nice when she's not hating me."

"She doesn't hate you. She's young still. Full of life and fight. Be careful you don't let her slip through your fingers by being... you know, you."

Foss poked one of the kanins with a stick to test its doneness. "Go tell Nik dinner's ready," he ordered Mace.

Charles stood with a morose expression.

"Don't give me that look," Foss grumbled. "It's your fault I had to carry his royal pain for two days straight. You're lucky I don't roast you on this spit. You're the errand boy until I say otherwise."

Charles left the circle to find Nik without a word.

I sat up, drawing Uncle Rick's eyes from the fire. "Lucy! Darling, how are you?" His gray beard could not mask his smile.

The others turned around, but Jens was on his feet and moving toward me. "Hey, you're awake. You feeling okay?"

I nodded as I sat up slowly, my neck stiff from sleeping on the ground. "Did all that really happen, then?"

Jens nodded, his dark eyes dancing with concern as he checked me over, looking at my eyeballs and testing the temperature of my hands. "When Mace gave you his Huldra whistle back at Nik's house, he put a command in there for you to feel elated. Happy." He kissed my forehead. "In his defense, he said he was worried about you after the Nøkkendalig and didn't want you to check out again. He's a little stronger at that whistle than he realized, or you're more susceptible to him or something. You were giddy until he put you to total relaxation, knocking you and Jamie both out until the first whistle wore off."

I pulled my knees up to my chest and shoved my head into my hands, totally embarrassed. "I didn't dream it, then? Was I really throwing myself at you like that?"

Jens nodded, his smirk unable to stay maturely hidden.

"That's so humiliating! I'm sorry, Jens."

"Maybe humiliating for you, but I'm pretty much the man over here. But how about the next time you want to sing a song about my muscles, stop calling them Jemima."

"Oh, jeez. I'm so sorry."

"You made it up to me by composing a dirty poem about my manhood. That was pretty entertaining. You even made Foss smile once. Didn't think that was possible."

I leaned forward into his shoulder and groaned. "Please forgive me. All of it. I'm so embarrassed."

Jens kissed the top of my head. "Oh, no. I'm holding you to everything for a long time. There's no end to the teasing you're getting for this."

"Shut up and kiss me," I begged, meeting his lips with

a tender stroke to replace the needy ones I'd showered him with earlier. "That feels a little better. Like us."

"For the record, I liked being attacked by you. I just wanted to make sure you knew what you were doing."

I laced my arms around his neck and exhaled my regret as we hugged each other. The fire was warm, and so was he. "I love you, you know."

He pressed his lips to my cheek. "You should. Not many guys'd be able to be a gentleman in that situation. I'm holding you to every dirty thing you said about me." He smiled into my cheek when I shivered. "After all, I'm the perfect man, according to you."

"Oh, shut up."

He tapped under my chin and raised my face to place a tender kiss on my lips. "I love you, too. I'm glad you're back."

"I'm glad you're you."

"Come on," he said, pulling me gently to my feet and leading me toward the fire. "Let's give Jamie a little more time to sleep it off before the best day of his life shatters."

"Oh, Britta!" I fretted, worried all over again. Jens lowered me carefully next to his sister as if I was just getting out of the hospital, and we held each other immediately. "I'm so sorry!"

Britta laughed softly, her hug tender and filled with her genuine love for me. "You didn't do anything to me to be sorry for. You were positively adorable. I've never been kissed that many times in my life."

"Not that. Well, yes, that. But the proposal! He finally let himself go, and it was like that? That's not how you pictured it."

Britta rubbed my back before releasing me. "You remember it, then? There's a chance he'll remember, too?"

I nodded, not looking forward to that conversation. "It feels like it all happened at a distance, but yeah. I remember everything."

Uncle Rick cleared his throat. "Lucy, I've already reprimanded Charles."

I leaned forward with my elbows on my knees and cradled my face with my hands. "What'd I miss while I was out?" I was too ashamed to make eye contact with any of the guys. I'm pretty sure I did a provocative dance to a Britney Spears song. No one should ever do that under any circumstances.

Uncle Rick pulled out his sack and fished through it. "Charles and I secured a *vatten liv*. It's a weed that helps you hold your breath for longer underwater. Hard to find, but not impossible with the right persuasion." He nodded to Jens. "It's been decided that Jens will take Nik down into Lugn River. The portal is at the very bottom, which isn't a problem for Nøkken. They can hold their breath upwards of twenty minutes underwater. But we would like Nik to remain unseen, so Jens will vanish him while he destroys the portal. The weed will solve the problem of Jens not being able to hold his breath that long."

"Oh, that's great!" I still kept my face hidden in my

hands and facing downward, too embarrassed to take in the damage I'd done.

"What, no song with our supper?" Tor teased. "I specifically remember ya promising me a song. Something livelier than tha one ya sang about Jens's eyebrows." He snapped his fingers to urge me to action.

Jens scratched his five o'clock shadow, giving me a sideways smile. "You went through a pretty vocal eighties hair band phase. Apparently I 'shook you all night long'."

I acted out dying of embarrassment, falling over in the grass.

Jens yanked me up. "Come on, Cherry Pie. Get some food in you. You keep missing whole days of eating. I don't like it. I like my baby with back."

I paled. "I didn't."

Jens laughed. "Oh, but you did. The whole rap. It was pretty impressive, actually. It's been a while since I've heard you sing that whole song. Luckily I was carrying you over my shoulder at that point, so you couldn't do your pop and lock." He stood up and did a perfect imitation of my best booty shaking, to the amusement of the crowd.

Nik's glimpse of lust was only caught by me, and he stuffed it back down before anyone could comment on it.

"Take it off!" I hollered, waving around my invisible dollar bills. Jens was a thing of beauty, shaking his backside to a beat only the two of us heard. I adored his sculpted physique, his heart that seemed cold at first, but was actually warm and open once you pried off the locks.

That night, it was his smile that did me in. I wondered how many moments he watched me from his unseen places, matching his smile to mine even though I never knew he was there. How lonely he must have been after Linus and my parents died. To watch someone going through the exact same thing, but not be able to commiserate with them must've been terrible.

As Jens shook his glorious backside to entertain us, I reached a new understanding of how deserving a moment must be to earn a smile from him. That he spent so many on me was a humbling thought, and I took that new knowledge with a readiness I had not possessed before.

"Is that really what yer world's like?" Tor inquired, skepticism stitching his eyebrows together.

Jens bowed to Nik's polite applause. "Pockets of it. You'll see." Jens sat back down at my side, sizing up my look of unmasked admiration hesitantly. "What?"

"It's you." I blinked at his confusion, unable to find eloquent words to communicate how much my heart filled and ached for him. "What a waste to've missed looking at you during the years you had to be invisible." I spoke slowly, and in that tiny moment, we knew the same language. "It's nice to see your face."

Jens snapped to attention, searching my sincere expression for signs of a joke. And just like that, he understood me as I was beginning to understand him. He cupped my cheeks, and with the greatest care, kissed my lips like he was making gentle love to them. When I was a pathetic puddle in his arms, he whispered, "That you see me now makes all the difference."

"Seems like your whole culture's a waste of time." Foss interrupted in his gruff manner. He slid the kanins off the spit, split them open and handed them around.

"And what all-noble vocation do you have, Foss? Does perpetual grouch pay well?" I said, only half-joking.

"I'm a retired mercenary. Now I own several ships that take in their share of fish." He bit into his bunny, letting the juices run down his chin. "Own a few dozen rats like you, too. They know how to keep their mouths shut in the company of men. A world of you? I can't imagine a more insolent and immature place. Let's hope I die well before then."

"Here's hoping," I replied with a piercing glare to my smile.

Jens barked out a rebuttal to the rotten man, but I placed my hand on his back to quiet him. I looked at Foss, conveying more disappointment in him than I could have communicated with a thousand words. "So we're back to that? Got it. You're big and scary and I hate you, too." I gave him a farewell salute. "It was fun while it lasted. You were almost redeemable."

"I care nothing for your redemption, little rat. At least that one knows her place." He motioned to Britta, who kept her eyes downward as she chewed. I wanted to pull a Jerry Springer and leap across the fire to strangle him for slighting Britta's sweetness.

Uncle Rick opened his mouth to correct Foss, but I shook my head. "Uh-uh. Don't worry about it, Uncle Rick. He's happy the way he is. We only have to last till the final portal falls. I can hold out until then." I fumed at Foss, tightening my grip on the slimy bunny meat. "But you'll watch how you talk about Britta. Say what you have to about me. I get it. But don't try your intimidation nonsense on her. She's too polite to take you down the way you need."

I barely saw it happen.

Britta's knife launched out, whipped across the fire and plunged strategically between Foss's spread knees. Britta stood, reminding them all she was a warrior, too. "Oh, dear sister. I'm not that polite." She picked up her head and glared – actually glared at the brute, who grumbled at being ganged up on by a couple of girls.

Foss stood, sword drawn. "You would dare attack one of the four powers? I could have you hanged for that!"

The others stood to intervene, but Britta didn't need the safeguard. Her voice rose with a hint of madness to it. "I'd like to see you try! They'll never hang me! They need someone to clean up their mess. Who would take my body down and prepare it for burial? Say what you want about my profession, but it affords me the same amount of untouchability as yours." Her upper lip curled. "All the kings and all the powers of Undraland love to fight, but no one wants to get their hands dirty."

Foss's logic was stuck in his throat, his mouth moving,

but no words daring to come out. "Know your place, rat," he finally spat.

Jens popped Foss in the chest with the flat of his hand. "Back down, Foss. My sister isn't your slave to jerk around however you feel like. Neither's Lucy." He held up his hands and addressed everyone. "Be cool, people. Finish your food and go to bed."

For the most part, everyone obeyed, reclaiming their space around the fire.

Britta bristled. "Excuse me. There's a man over there who doesn't seem to mind my presence." Britta's eyes watched Jamie stirring a few yards away. She took two portions over to him so they could have a minute alone.

Jens looked like he wanted to go check on his friend, but I tugged him down next to me. "Give them some time."

"I... yeah. You're right."

"Eat with me."

Jens tapped his kanin leg to mine with that half-smile I adored. "It's a date."

24

FIGHTING AMONGST THE RANKS

We walked for two more days after that. Two days of Tor explaining the process of maturing the perfect batch of Gar. Two days of listening to Nik retell the history of the Nøkken for my benefit. Two days of learning more about Mace and his lonely childhood. Two days of holding Jens's hand like a true couple off on a nature walk together. Two days of Jamie building up his courage to do the same with Britta.

It was also two days of Foss treating Britt and me like dirt. He even knocked me down once when Jens and Henry Mancini were with Uncle Rick and Charles gathering more supplies in a nearby village. No apology. No help back up. Martin Luther King would have been proud that I did not choke him – not that I could reach his granite neck anyway.

The thing of it was that I could see a flicker of

conscience each time he was terrible. Charles peeling off the curse was working, but the behavior was so ingrained that he would have to start making conscious choices to break old habits if he ever wanted to make real progress. It was to the point where he could begin to choose the kind of man he wanted to be, instead of the curse choosing for him. I decided to tread lightly to make the choice easier for him.

"You'll not be rough with her like that anymore, Foss," Britta demanded when he knocked me down again ten minutes later.

Foss and I were so shocked she said anything, we both just stared at her for a second. "How dare you speak to me like that, Tomten scum!" Foss postured, his chest so wide, I had to remind myself not to cower.

"No! It's fine. I tripped, Britt. Foss would never do something so mean."

"I know you're lying," Britta argued, her chin raised in defiance.

Jamie, Nik and Tor were a ways behind and finally caught up. Nik gave me a hand up and brushed the dirt off my backside. "What's going on?"

Before Foss or Britta could chime in with their cacophony of contradictory opinions, I held up my hands. "Clumsy moment."

"Why are you sticking up for him?" Britta demanded. She turned to Jamie. "Foss has been –"

I cut her off for the sake of peace among the ranks. "I

love you, too, Britt. We're not going to get anywhere if we keep fighting, though. So I'm putting a stop to it. He can't use me to start fights anymore. We're a team, and if we're all going to make it out of this, we have to start working together." I glared at Foss. "So this is me, working with you, Foss. Being the big mercenary boss is easy. Working with people you hate is hard." He started to argue, but I shook my head, raising my fist in the air. "Prove you're stronger than me, Foss! Prove you're strong enough to do something actually hard for you. Get along with us for the rest of the trip. It'll be the hardest thing you've ever had to do, I'm sure, but Alrik didn't ask you on this trip because he thought you took the easy way out." He started to interrupt, but I waved my arms to silence him. "Newsflash, it's time to either man up or show everyone what a childish rat *you* are!"

The tension was too high. The next move was his, and we were all watching him make the choice of manliness or childish behavior.

He sneered at the pickle I put him in. Then he responded in a way I had not anticipated. Foss raised his enormous arm and backhanded me, sending me flying into the grass.

Britta shrieked, her hands over her mouth.

Jamie spat blood from his mouth at Foss and socked him one as I blinked back my tears. "You hit her, you hit a Tomten prince, you fool! I could have you in the stocks for that! My family could wage war on the Fossegrimens for one of the four powers attacking the Tonttu throne!"

"I don't play mind games with children," Foss snarled. When he saw Tor standing at Jamie's side and Nik kneeling in front of me, he realized he did not have an ally. I was just glad Jens had Henry Mancini. I don't think my temper could've taken it if he'd acted out on my dog. Nik held my hair back and rubbed my back as I spat blood on the grass.

Britta was shaking with rage. Watching her slowly unhinge her grip on servility was unsettling. Only I saw the dip into her apron pocket. I shouted for her to stop, but her mind was made up. Britta had wild eyes and steady hands capable of preparing bodies for death from the noose. Her knife flew out from her and sunk into the top of the hand Foss struck me with.

He roared. I screamed. It was chaos.

"Sing, Nik! Calm them down," I ordered, struggling to get to my feet. I ran to Foss, showing him my hands were gentle and would only try to help him.

To his credit, he only grunted once when I slid the blade out of his hand.

To my credit, I didn't barf all over the wound, which started oozing thick blood the second the air hit it.

I washed his hand with water from my canteen, hoping beyond hope that he wouldn't take his pain out on me. "Easy, Foss." He was a bear ready to strike. I kept my voice quiet, slicing the tension with silk instead of a chainsaw. "Britta's the meekest girl I've ever met, and you turned her into that." I shook my head. "You have a choice to make. Be under the curse of your people, or be the best of your kind." Then I took the knife, giving him a look that warned him to trust me. He stiffened, but didn't stop the blade as I cut off his shirt sleeve. "For what it's worth, I have faith in you." Then I wrapped the cloth around his hand, making a tight bandage.

Foss flexed his hand, wincing at the pain. "I care nothing for your faith."

I waited a few beats for Nik's song to soothe sense into Foss. Then I took a chance and kissed his temple, shocking him out of his bull-headedness. "Be good to me," I admonished him. "Don't settle for being one of the four powers. Be big enough to be the only one." I wrapped my arms around his neck when I saw him debating whether to be man or beast. To my surprise and his, he leaned for a moment into my lips, his body begging for one more kind kiss. I indulged him, running my fingers through his short hair. "That's the faith I have in you. I won't make you weak. I'll make you the strongest."

Nik continued to sing quietly, erasing the animosity by small degrees every few bars. Shoulders began to relax, and though everyone was still mad, there was less of a chance of someone flying off the handle.

Foss stood abruptly, breaking out of my embrace. "Get away from me, rat."

I wanted to shake sense into him, if such a thing were

possible. I realized in that moment of my life that change was not in the cards for everyone. Foss might never become a better person, and the world would not shine as bright in his corner of it.

I took a deep breath and recited my favorite historical figure's famous speech under my breath like a prayer. "'In the process of gaining our rightful place, we must not be guilty of wrongful deeds. Let us not seek to satisfy our thirst for freedom by drinking from the cup of bitterness and hatred. We must forever conduct our struggle on the high plane of dignity and discipline. We must not allow our creative protest to degenerate into physical violence.'"

Nik helped me to my feet and smoothed his thumb over my sore cheek, kissing it once as he held me. I brushed the hair off my shoulders and donned an authoritative tone. "No one tells Jens, Alrik or Mace a thing about this. I won't have Foss win this by stirring up more anger and more fighting in the group. It stops here. We all stop fighting today. Taking down Pesta should be more important to you than taking me or Britt down, Foss. Make your choice. Pesta or me."

Foss seethed, his answer stuck in his throat.

"Good enough. Let's get going. They're supposed to meet us at that giant hill, and it feels like it keeps getting further away as more stupidity sneaks into the group." I laced my arm through Britta's, my cheek still throbbing. I dropped her knife back into her apron. "You okay, Jamie?"

Jamie looked like a bull ready to charge. All notion of a

lackadaisical life spent wearing a crown and eating bonbons felt like a joke when seeing him in this light. He was no man for sitting on a throne. He was a beast for killing bears and taking out mercenaries.

"Let's move," Jamie seethed.

Nik kissed my cheek again, lacing his fingers through mine as we walked. "A queen if I ever saw one." His hand on mine was sweet, sure, but there was a note of territorial claim to it.

I kept a healthy distance from Foss. Jamie and I stayed close to Britta, not ready to risk her safety on Foss's cruel nature. I guessed it would not take long to break our feeble alliance.

25

NIK THE MAN OF VALOR

Our group reunited with Uncle Rick's team, and we walked another day. The gorgeous prairie that days ago enthralled me was now kinda, well, boring. But I would take boring any day over Weres or spiders, so I didn't complain.

Nik's puffed-up chest and swagger began to melt as we neared the lake that contained the portal. Jens was holding my hand and Nik's. The Tomtens were vanishing us so we could get closer without being seen. Nik's eyes were dull with thoughts of losing the life he'd made for himself, however veiled that life may be.

"You okay?" I asked of his cloudy demeanor.

Nik shrugged. "As okay as I can be. I fear I've lost your optimism in all this." He pointed to the side of the lake, where we could see in the distance too many blue and white-haired soldiers flanking the water. "They've called in security. There didn't used to be any guards here. I count three dozen now." He paled, his mouth falling open at the overly muscled, tall Fossegrimen man in the center. "Is that... How did the Mouthpiece know? How did he follow us here? I thought he was going the opposite direction."

Even though I was invisible, I shrank behind Jens. I'd never known the fear of being hunted, but the goose bumps all over my body told me it was not a thing one got used to.

I examined the structure sticking out from the center of the lake. It was a rock sculpture twice the size of Foss. I squinted and made out the shape of an enormous fish coming up out of the water on a plank, its tail swishing in triumph. It sort of looked like it was on a seesaw.

A salmon on a seesaw. *Salmon Seesaw.* I gasped at the secret family password brought to life before me. I ran my finger over Linus's ashes, wishing he could be here to see it with me, holy crapping in unison as we usually did when something blew our minds.

"What do you need from us?" Jens cast around like an army general, looking for weak points and forming a plan of attack.

"The rake and some space, I guess. Jens, you shouldn't come down with me. I know Alrik found you that weed, but as soon as I start tearing down the portal, they're going to know I'm there. They'll attack with their tritons, and you'll get hit. Whether they can see us or not, they'll know where to lunge."

Jens nodded. "I know, but you'll never get past their line if they can see you with the rake. I guess you'll just have to be quick about destroying the portal once we get down there. Then swim us out as fast as you can."

I really didn't like this plan, but as I had nothing better, I kept out of it.

When we got a little closer, our party stopped behind a thick smattering of trees that kept us safely hidden. Jens kicked off his boots and shoved them in his red pack, turning me over to Jamie for vanishing. Britta kissed Nik's cheek and her brother's, and then it was handed to me to continue our little tradition. I stood up on my toes and kissed Nik, rubbing his cheek to mine. "Be safe, Nik. We'll give you a real hero's welcome when you come back."

Nik brushed his lips to mine, and then whispered against my mouth, "Be brave, Queen Lucy. Thank you for our tawdry night together. You are a treasure, indeed."

Jens took out the rake from his magic bag and handed it to Nik. My favorite Nøkken shook hands with the men, eyeing them as an equal, instead of someone pretending to be so.

Jens looked to me for his send off, but again I refused him. "You and I don't say goodbye. Not until it's true."

Jens nodded, his expression resolute as he shifted to focusing on the task at hand. Uncle Rick handed him the weed, which he held off on choking down until just before dipping into the water.

Jens put his hand on the back of my neck, gripping me

tight as he took control of the group. "Alright, here's how it works. Everyone goes toward the docks. No one's going to jump in and try to fight with us or for us. You're all going to the docks. Nik and I'll meet you there in one hour. If we're not there in one hour, gank a boat and leave for Fossegrimen."

My head jerked in his direction. "What? You're not seriously suggesting we leave you behind."

Jens gripped me harder, begging me without words to fall in line and respect his expertise. "That's exactly what I'm saying. Nik and I can row a boat as good as anyone and catch up to you at the first opportunity. Go to Foss's house and we'll all meet there." He stuck his hand out to Jamie. "If I don't make it, I'm trusting you to be Lucy's Tom."

My head whipped from Jamie to Jens as my fate was exchanged by way of a handshake. "What? Jens, don't talk like that! Jamie's not my Tom! It's you or no one!"

Jamie pulled Jens in for a tight hug and a kiss on either cheek. "I'll keep her safe until my very last breath, brother." The hug could've ended there, but Jens held on a few seconds longer. I could tell in the tightness with which he gripped his best friend that he was anxious about this portal.

Jens released Jamie, delivered a brief kiss to the top of my head without looking me in the eye, and grabbed Nik's shoulder, his machete drawn.

Jamie reached for my hand to vanish me, but I yanked away from his advance. "No! This is a terrible plan!"

Lucy, do you trust Jens?

I steamed at Jamie's question. *Of course! But this isn't right. Don't you feel it?*

If you trust him, let him lead.

The look I gave Jamie was nothing to be trifled with, and he took the nonverbal admonition with grace. "Let's go, *liten syster.*"

"Little sister?" I inquired.

Jamie nodded, holding onto Tor with his other hand while Foss clamped down on his shoulder. I scooped up Henry Mancini, who nuzzled my chin and licked my face. Britta vanished Uncle Rick and Charles, looking a perfect mix of scared and fierce.

We set off in our direction, and I tried not to grow anxious with every step we took away from Jens.

We were a quarter of the way to the meeting place when we heard it. I turned my head to see the scope of the commotion near the pool. My eyes were wide when I saw Nøkken diving into the water with their menacing tritons sharpened for a swift kill. We all turned to watch, helpless to do anything.

Uncle Rick was giving a command to Jamie, but I was so focused on the lake, I did not hear it. Suddenly Jamie was leading an invisible me, Foss and Tor in haste toward the docks while Britta ran Uncle Rick and Charles toward the water.

"What's going on?" I demanded, not liking Charles so

near the danger. Henry Mancini could sense my fear as I held him to my chest.

Jamie did not answer – a sign that he was engrossed in the new plan. He only plodded us all forward at his quickened pace.

Tor replied, "We're outnumbered. Alrik and tha halfy're gonna see if they can help get them out."

I had a million questions as I trotted along with my head twisted so I could catch glimpses of the lake. I nearly jumped out of my skin a few seconds later when water shot straight up from the lake fifteen feet in the air. It was a wave that went nowhere, but remained tall like a wall until it went plunging straight below, turning itself inside out. Nøkken were thrown out of the lake by the fistful as the red light that signaled the portal was being broken shot up out of the water like an explosive.

The Mouthpiece was shouting orders, whipping his head around as he fumed. He stalked back and forth along the edge of the lake, his dogged search for me made me cling tight to Jamie.

I made several noises of worry and fear when I did not see signs of Nik or Jens. The water thrashed and crashed around the edges of the lake, giving the two plenty of time to finish the job. Uncle Rick and Charles had a firm grasp on their control of the water when they worked together.

When the red light ceased, we knew the portal was destroyed. The Nøkken were focused on the big eruptions of water, but I was zeroing in on the perimeter, waiting for small ripples to let me know that Jens and Nik were on their way back to us.

Tor and Foss were deliberating about the size of the aquatic upset. "There's no way that's Alrik. Elves can do a fair amount ta the water, but I've never seen nothing like that."

"It's that Mace. When he scrambled the rat's brains, his spell was too powerful. This is him. First his Huldra abilities are too much, and now his Elfish ones, too? Where'd Alrik find this guy?"

Tor's eyes were wide as he took in the water wall that was building at least two stories tall, and growing. "I don't know, but I'm starting ta be grateful he's on this trip. Had no idea halfies were so useful."

We watched and waited on the path between the forest and the docks for far too long. "Something's gone wrong. They should've been back by now," Jamie ruled.

All of a sudden, three Nøkken guards broke through the water chaos, hefting a body onto the grass.

There was blood. Too much blood painted the body that I had held only a handful of nights ago. His body was splayed at an unnatural angle, arm twisted too far above his head to be attached properly. My mouth opened, but Foss's hand cupped it. He didn't need to. I had no voice to scream with.

White-blue hair now slicked red, Nik was rolled out and dragged by his ankles. The Mouthpiece bent down and checked his pulse. His commanding voice boomed out, "We got him! It's Nik the Man of Valor! He's dead. Find the rake! Bring me the rake and look for Queen Lucy! If we've got Nik, she can't be far! Queen Lucy must be brought in for questioning. She's been seen traveling with Nik."

Foss's hand was still clamped around my mouth, but he drew me back and pressed me against his firm torso, posturing to prove I was protected.

My heart sank as seconds passed without movement from the mangled mess that was Nik. I shook away from Foss's stern grip on my face. "We have to do something!" I whispered, tears running down my face. Henry Mancini licked my cheeks, but it brought me no comfort.

"We do nothing now," Foss ruled in his finite way.

"But he's not dying as a hero! He's going out as a criminal! There's no redemption in this. He won't get the respect he deserves."

Foss covered my mouth again, only this time, it was not as forceful. "This is the way it is for true heroes. They go out for the job, not the glory."

I willed with everything in me for Nik to move one muscle, to give me a sign that he was alive to some extent.

But Nik did not move. He did not breathe. There was no more happiness in his haughty eyes. There was no more grief in his heart for Kirk. As I looked out at Nik in the distance, I found there was no more of Nik at all. Pesta would not get his soul, but neither would we.

26

SPLITTING UP

"Shut down the roads out of town!" the Mouthpiece called to his team.

Foss and Jamie exchanged troubled glances. "We can't wait," Foss ruled. "They're going to shut down the docks when they don't find the rake, and we'll be stuck here."

Jamie nodded. "Sure, but what's our other option?"

Tor said what Jamie could not. "The two portals left ta shut down are the Fossegrimens and humans."

I pushed Foss's hand away from my mouth. "And the elves."

Tor readied his ax. "Right. I'm not needed, so I'll wait fer tha others and help if I can. I'll let them know ya've gone on."

My head darted around between the men. "Wait, what? Splitting up wasn't part of the plan!"

Something caught my eye at the edge of the lake. My intake of breath was just enough warning for Foss to cover my mouth again before I let out a horrified scream.

A body rose to the surface of the water, surrounded by a pool of blood.

"It's probably not Jens," Jamie insisted, his voice pinched with anxiety.

Tor shooed us away. "We'll catch up once tha search dies down. Go! This might be yer only chance ta get ta the Fossegrimens. Maybe ya can find a few sympathizers and gain some allies." Tor was already shaking Foss's hand. "We'll grab tha rake and meet ya there as soon as we can."

"No!" I argued, my blood cold as my eyes zeroed in on the body. The black shirt was shifting to and fro with the current, but I couldn't see the victim's hair. *Black or bluish white? Black or bluish white? Come on!* I shouted in my head. "We can't just leave Jens and everyone to fend for themselves!"

Jamie hugged Tor with trembling arms and kissed both his cheeks. "Farewell, Torsten the Mighty. We'll see you soon."

"But you'll be seen!" I pointed out. "Jamie can't vanish you if we leave."

Tor shrugged. "What's the crime in a dwarf visiting tha lovely Nøkken countryside? I certainly don't have no rake on me. I wouldn't be suspect ta them anyway. Dwarves don't swim. Free pass for Torsten the Mighty." He reached out and gently pried Henry Mancini from my arms, giving me a stern look when I resisted.

Panic built up in me. "But he's mine! Don't take my dog! I'll keep him quiet, I swear!"

"Now, now. Don't ya worry. I'll keep watch over him. Ya might have ta sneak off the docks, in which case ya'll have better luck if yer yap stays with me."

Henry Mancini licked Tor's beard and then sneezed, whining at me to question whether I thought this was the best way for him. I ran my hands over my puppy's fur, trying to put on a brave face underneath my tears. "It's okay, Henry Mancini. Mommy's just going on a little trip. I'll be back to come get you sooner than you think." I nuzzled the top of his head, my heart breaking as he whined. "I'll always come back for you."

"Off ya go, lass."

"Tor, I don't like this idea," I insisted, my heart pounding as I cast around for any excuse they might allow me to stay. "Jens! The body in the lake... It's... I don't know if... We can't leave without Jens!"

Before I knew what was happening, Tor pulled me down to his level, which was only a handful of stooped inches, and kissed my mouth. "Fare thee well, Queen Lucy the Brave."

Then Jamie all but dragged me away from Tor and Henry Mancini. He took me away from Uncle Rick, my new brother and my new best friend. He led me away from

Nik's ripped and lonely body that would not be laid to rest with any respect, nor with Kirk.

Of all things, he took me away from Jens.

Love *Nøkken*? Leave a review!

27

FOSSEGRIM

Enjoy a free preview of *Fossegrim*,
Book three in the Undraland Series.

oss shook his head as he, Jamie and I ran away from the lake where the Nøkken portal to the Land of Be had just been destroyed by Nik. "We stick to the plan. Let's head for the docks. As soon as Alrik and Charles stop fiddling with the water, Tor will grab them and they'll meet us in Fossegrim." We were holding hands so Jamie could vanish us, which made for an awkward escape.

"What if they need our help?" I argued as we ran toward the ocean. Well, I ran. They trotted, their long legs making the trek far easier on them. "How can you be sure that bloody body we saw floating to the surface wasn't Jens?"

Jamie's steps faltered, but Foss righted him. Foss's response was firm. "Nøkken have the upper hand in a water fight. If we get involved, it'll mean death for us all. Those who can be of use are helping. We're sticking to the plan. Let's go."

I wanted to run back to Nik and Jens, but part of me saw the merit in Foss's logic. I wasn't even the best swimmer in gym class. And tritons? Those Nøkken were no joke. Plus, given my last experience when the Nøkkendalig attacked me underwater, I wasn't keen on getting back in a lake so soon.

Jens was probably fine. He had Uncle Rick, Charles, Britta and Tor. They would find him and help him. His body probably wasn't the one I saw with blood blooming out into the water in red puffs, streaking through the blue in ribbons. I felt cold and empty. The limbo of not knowing felt like a vice around my throat.

When we reached the dock, Foss took the lead. Jamie kept me vanished outside a small shanty just off the dock while Foss negotiated a small boat for us to cross the water in.

I had no idea Undraland was so vast. I heard Foss talking with the merchant, and he pointed to a piece of land so far away, it was barely visible. The dock worker had a fear of Foss that went beyond being intimidated by his physical appearance. Foss's reputation had preceded him. Whatever softening had happened as a result of Mace's whistle stripping away layers of his curse, it was pushed out by his sneer that seemed even more cruel than usual.

Foss paid the man, who began loading into the small boat the baskets Foss pointed to. There was a basket of food, one with blankets and clothes, one with nets, and a few I could not tell what was inside.

When Foss gave us a discreet nod, we made our way invisibly to the dock with quiet feet. Jamie lowered me down and Foss steadied me with his hands on my hips. I didn't love the fact that since I was the smallest of our trio, I was to sit on the floor between the two wooden seats. I curled my knees to my chest to make room for the invisible man.

The image of surely not Jens bleeding out in the water imprinted itself on the inside of my eyelids, taunting me whenever I drew breath. Since I was invisible and no one would see my miniature breakdown, I turned my head to the side and wept into Jamie's thigh.

Jamie ran his hands through my blonde tangles. "There, there. Nik knew this was a possibility. We all did going into it. There wasn't time for him to suffer much, and we must be grateful for that."

"Grateful? We have no idea if Jens is even alive! Nik's body surfaced, but Jens went down there invisible. If he's dead, will we even know? How will they find his body?"

Jamie gripped my hair too hard to be comforting.

"When Tomten die, our magic leaves us, so he'll be easy to spot."

"That's it? That's all you can say? He's your best friend!"

Jamie didn't answer, but looked far off into the distance. Through the psychic bond we shared, I could tell he was not anxious to reach our destination, but more nervous for what happened when we did. "It's best we remain concealed in the land of the Fossegrimens. They don't value women as your culture does."

"Okay," I answered, forsaking open grieving and turning inward.

Jens could be dead right now. The invisible force I'd taken for granted was gone. I had hope that he would survive, but no assurances. I was more connected to Jamie than to him, and I really hated that. If he died, would I feel the ping? Would I know across an ocean in my heart that he stopped existing? Would the pounding in my chest feel hollow, or would I keep hoping for his return, eternally pining in my state of relationship limbo?

I was so tired of surviving. I rested against Jamie's thigh between his legs and closed my eyes, pretending the hand in my hair wasn't to vanish me, but to bring me comfort. I had to do a lot of pretending lately. I could feel Jamie's angst through our psychic bond, which only compounded my own.

Foss rowed us across the water toward the docks. As we got closer, the landscape changed. Instead of the vivid green of Nøkken with its gorgeous flowers and bursting nature, Fossegrim was only sparsely green with muted sand and limited foliage along the outskirts of the island. There were beige tents set up along the coastline with various merchants selling their wares. It was Aladdin's town from the cartoon I always thought was a little too racy to be for children.

Foss took charge, correctly sensing Jamie and I were useless in our current state. "You'll stay here. I'll send Viggo for you. He'll bring you to my house where we'll wait. Stay hidden until you get to my bedroom." He snapped his finger to make sure we were paying attention, since he couldn't see us. "Not my property. Not my house. My bedroom. If the Mouthpiece catches wind of you on Fossegrim soil, you'll be easy to find. He won't set foot on our land, but we don't want him to know that you have. The less people know you're here, the better. I have business to attend to, and then I'll be home."

Jamie agreed for the both of us, since Foss couldn't give a crap what I thought anyway. *Sure, let's split the group further. It's clearly proved a solid idea. Whatever. At least I get Jamie.*

Foss had rowed us for nearly three hours. I was just starting to get over my slight seasickness when we docked. "Lucy, where's your face?" Foss asked, reaching around near his knees.

"Right here," I said, hoping he could follow my voice and wouldn't have to pat me on the top of my head like a dog.

He did it anyway, and I cringed.

He bent his neck to try looking me in the eye. What he couldn't see was me obstinately looking toward the heavens. *Take that.*

"Look, rat. Jens and your world tolerate you better than I do or my people will. If you want to get out of this intact, you'll keep your mouth shut and your head down. You'll get a change of clothes from Viggo when you get to my house. Keep your head down like your maidenhood depends on it. They've never seen a blonde before."

"Don't talk about my virginity," I scolded, clutching tighter to Jamie's thigh. I took a breath and softened a little, since Foss was actually trying to be helpful. "But I can do that. Thanks for the heads up. No one ever tells me what to expect when we get to a new country."

His expression was a snarl, as it usually was. "I'm not doing it for you. I owe Jens more than he'll hold me to, and I don't like having debts. I'm keeping you safe for his sake."

"Aw, shucks. You say the sweetest things."

When Foss got out of the boat, it was like losing a small elephant and a giant dark cloud. The boat floated at least a foot higher, and I felt like I could breathe well enough to feel the grief from leaving Jens and Nik behind.

Read *Fossegrim*,
the next book in the series.

ABOUT THE AUTHOR

USA Today bestselling author Mary E. Twomey lives in Michigan with her three adorable children. She enjoys reading, writing, vegetarian cooking, and telling her children fantastic stories about wombats.

While she loves writing fantasy, dystopian, and paranormal tales for her readers, Mary also writes romance under the name Tuesday Embers, and cozy mysteries under the name Molly Maple.

Visit her online at www.maryetwomey.com, and sign up for her newsletter, so you never miss a new release.

9 781088 176436